Praise for *Colorful*

"Certain books, you know the ones, get under your skin. I was extraordinarily moved by Eto Mori's *Colorful*. It was as if Makoto was speaking directly into my own ear in the dark. This intimate, brave novel has already been read by millions in Japan. It cries out to be read by millions more."

—PETER ORNER, author of *Maggie Brown & Others*

"Eto Mori's *Colorful* is ingenious, funny, and offers razor-keen insights into adult lives. It will captivate English language readers as it has millions of Japanese."

—KATHERINE GOVIER, author of *The Printmaker's Daughter* and *The Ghost Brush*

"Through Jocelyne Allen's translation of the Japanese classic *Colorful*, author Eto Mori invites a new generation of readers to view the coming-of-age experience, though rife with travails, with heart and good humor. Whether in Japan or the United States, readers will find space in these pages to laugh, reflect—and keep breathing."

—KIT FRICK, author of *See All the Stars* and *I Killed Zoe Spanos*

"Unlike anything I've ever read before, *Colorful* is a fresh and bold story that asks big and important questions about death, mental health, and most important, what it means to truly live. Makoto is a singular character whose struggles will be deeply relatable to many young people. A truly special novel." —JASMINE WARGA, author of *Other Words for Home*, a Newbery Honor Book, and *My Heart and Other Black Holes*

"In this welcome and timely translation, American readers meet Makoto, a modern-day Holden Caulfield who has had it with academic pressure, social rejection, and family expectations. His page-turning adventures are both caustic and tender, and entirely real, and his journey teaches that even if we're kind of a mess, we're still doing our best and that's what matters. Colorful is ultimately an outstretched hand to young adults. It delivers the most craved-for reassurance: *you're okay, and you are not alone.*"

—JULIE LYTHCOTT-HAIMS, *New York Times* bestselling author of *How to Raise an Adult*

COLORFUL

COLORFUL

A Novel

ETO MORI

Translated from the Japanese by
JOCELYNE ALLEN

COUNTERPOINT
BERKELEY, CALIFORNIA

COLORFUL

Library of Congress Cataloging-in-Publication Data
Names: Mori, Eto, 1968– author. | Allen, Jocelyne, 1974– translator.
Title: Colorful : a novel / Eto Mori ; translated from the Japanese by
    Jocelyne Allen.
Other titles: Karafuru. English
Description: First counterpoint edition. | Berkeley, California :
    Counterpoint, 2021.
Identifiers: LCCN 2020023786 | ISBN 9781640094420 (paperback)
    | ISBN 9781640094437 (ebook)
Classification: LCC PL873.O75 K3713 2020 | DDC 895.63/6—dc23
LC record available at https://lccn.loc.gov/2020023786

Cover design by Christopher Lin
Book design by Wah-Ming Chang

COUNTERPOINT
2560 Ninth Street, Suite 318
Berkeley, CA 94710
www.counterpointpress.com

Counterpoint gratefully acknowledges the support from the Japan
Foundation for this publication.

Printed in the United States of America

10 9 8 7 6 5 4 3 2 1

COLORFUL

PROLOGUE

As my dead soul leisurely drifted off to some dark place, this angel I'd never seen before suddenly appeared right in my way.

"Congratulations! You've won the lottery!" The angel smiled. He gave me this speech:

"You committed a grave error before you died. Hence, your soul is now culpable. Generally, you would be disqualified at this time and removed from the cycle of rebirth. Which is to say, you would never be reborn again. However, more than a few consider this to be a barbaric taking of life, and so our boss occasionally gives lottery winners a second chance, as it were. You are one such lucky soul! Against all odds, you've won that lottery!"

I wasn't quite happy with this sudden news. If I'd had eyes, I would've opened them wide in surprise, and if I'd had a mouth, I would've dropped my jaw and gaped. But I was nothing more than a formless soul. It was strange enough that I could hear the angel's voice and see him there before me. He looked just like a regular human being, a tall man with beautiful, delicate features, his slim body draped in white fabric. He had the wings on his back, at any rate, but I couldn't see a halo on his head.

"Thanks for the offer," I said. "But I'll pass."

"And why is that?"

"Just because." I'd already forgotten everything about my previous existence. When I spoke to the angel, my voice sounded masculine, so I figured I was a guy, but I had absolutely no memory of what kind of guy or what sort of life I'd led. All that stayed with me was this vague weariness, this total disinterest in ever going back to the world below. "Because I don't want to. You know that thing where someone wanders into a department store and then this big ball pops open over their head and confetti falls all over the place, and it's all, Congratulations! You're the one millionth customer! And everyone's making this whole big fuss and forcing this trip to Hawaii on them right then and there? That's what this feels like. I just want to stay home and sleep."

"I do understand what you're saying." The angel calmly accepted my complaint. "Between the two of us, those of us who work upstairs also have our fair share of doubts about this lottery method. Unfortunately, however, the boss's decisions are final. Neither you nor I—nor anyone else, for that matter—can disobey his word. He is, after all, the father of all creation."

Colorful

I couldn't really say anything when he came at me like that. I had a mean one on my hands here. I was forced into silence.

"Besides." The angel's bright blue eyes glittered ominously. "What awaits you is absolutely, most certainly not a Hawaiian paradise."

The angel's name was Prapura. He was a guide, currently in charge of me. His job now was to take me to the place where I would have my second chance.

But a second chance at what exactly?

In that place between heaven and earth, I tried to get my head around what was going on, while the angel went ahead to give me the rough overview of things pre-departure.

The gist of it all was:

1. My soul had made a pretty serious mistake in my previous life. Normally, I wouldn't get to be reborn again, but fortunately, I'd won the lottery and a chance for a do-over.

2. A do-over meant that I would go back for training in the world below, the place where I failed in my previous life.

3. Training meant that my soul would borrow someone else's body down there for a fixed period of time. Prapura's boss would decide on the body and the family I would stay with.

4. In angel industry slang, this training was referred to as a "homestay."

5. Of course, the family you ended up with could be hit or miss. For every good family, there was an awful one. For every tragedy, a comedy. I could even end up in a violent home. But the size of my crime in my previous life determined my new home, so I could complain all I wanted, but I wouldn't have a leg to stand on. (Damn . . .)

6. Prapura would help me with any problems I had during the homestay. But how much help he was would depend on his mood.

7. If I made good progress with the training, at a certain point I would get back my memories of my previous life. The instant I realized how big my mistake had been, the homestay would be over. My soul would leave the borrowed body and move on to whatever came next, safely restored to the cycle of rebirth. Hoorah, huzzah, basically. (Seriously?)

"That's essentially how this will proceed, Makoto." Prapura had no sooner wrapped up his little lecture than he was twitching his wings, impatiently. "Now, let us make our way to the world below."

"Makoto?"

"From this moment on, you will be Makoto Kobayashi. He attempted suicide by overdose three days ago, and he remains in critical condition. Just between us, he's going to die soon without ever regaining consciousness. The moment his soul slips out, you will step inside."

"So you're saying," I started, "I'm stealing his body?"

"Don't be so morbid!" Prapura snapped. "Please think of it more as you'll be taking care of his body for a short while. Let's have a positive attitude here, shall we?"

"So what's this Makoto Kobayashi like?"

"You'll find out once you become him."

I would've liked a little more advance prep, but Prapura already had his wings fully deployed. He looked extremely fed up with all this talk. He yanked on my arm and flew upward, dragging me along with him.

The floor abruptly dropped out from under me, and then we were plummeting downward at the speed of light. Prapura's wings didn't seem to be doing much of anything. Was he really an angel? Or was he a demon? I suddenly got very nervous, but then I lost consciousness and was swallowed up by a swirling vortex of brilliant color.

1

When I came to, I was Makoto Kobayashi. I had this total physical sensation of "you got a body for real, right here." My soul, which had been naked an instant before, was now wrapped in flesh like a heavy coat. The flesh seemed to be lying on a futon. No, wait, a bed. The place stank of disinfectant, too, so maybe a hospital bed? And then I remembered that Makoto had tried to commit suicide. He was supposed to be in critical condition or something... Hm? I could hear someone crying. Who?

Before I'd taken even half a second to brace myself for what I'd find, I opened my eyes and found a middle-aged lady sobbing helplessly.

"Makoto," the lady murmured, dazed. Then she shrieked, "Makoto?!"

I could feel the other human shadows in the room all turn toward me at the same time. I indeed appeared to be in a hospital room—an array of grim medical devices stood on either side of the bed, and the white uniforms of nurses flitted in and out of sight on the other sides of the machines.

"It can't be," someone groaned, and then the white shadows were bustling around the room.

"Makoto!" a middle-aged man shouted, as he propped the lady up. "He came back! He's alive!!"

Later, I found out that Makoto Kobayashi had been pronounced dead just ten minutes earlier. His spirit had risen up to wherever it was off to, so I'd slipped into his vacated body and popped his eyes open. No *wonder* they were shocked. Who wouldn't be?

"Heartbeat . . . Blood pressure . . . I can't believe this!" Even the doctor got caught up in the excitement.

The woman and the man were over the moon at Makoto's resurrection. It was obvious that they were his parents. Of course they were wild with joy—their dead son had just come back to life. They cried out silently as they stroked my cheeks, rubbed my arms, hugged my whole body. It was strange but I wasn't bothered by these complete strangers getting all grabby with me. Makoto's body was taking it all in ahead of my mind.

There was one more person in Makoto's family. A boy in a school uniform at the foot of the bed, shoulders squared, glaring at me with bloodshot eyes. While everyone else in the room—the parents, the doctor, the nurses— was celebrating, he was the only one acting too cool for school. This was Makoto's older brother, Mitsuru, a fact I would only learn much later. Right now, though, I didn't know how old Makoto was, let alone Mitsuru, so I wondered hazily if the glaring kid was a brother or something.

"Makoto, you made it back. Makoto! Makoto!" The half-crazed father repeating his son's name over and over.

The mother clinging to my body, refusing to let go.

The brother, intensely aloof.

Although I wasn't exactly in a position for careful observation, I had at least come face to face with the family I'd be staying with. They didn't look particularly rich or like one of them was a celebrity. But given the spiteful look that angel gave me, I hadn't expected much to begin with. Still, at first glance, they seemed like normal people, and I decided to chalk that up as a win. I mean, it was plenty possible that when I opened my eyes, I could have been surrounded by eight macho men in red-and-yellow-striped leotards, weeping profusely over my prone body. Nothing better than average when it comes to life in general.

The instant I relaxed a bit, I was overcome with a sudden sleepiness. Makoto hadn't left his body in the best shape when he died back there. I was bogged down by this sluggish feeling; I couldn't make the body move too well. Eventually, I dropped off without saying so much as a word.

And so went my debut as Makoto Kobayashi.

The sluggish, drowsy feeling continued for a while. Makoto's body recovered so well and so quickly that his doctor nearly vibrated with delight. But maybe because of the medication they gave me three times a day, I was still constantly sleepy and the body felt so heavy around me. This didn't strike me as such a bad thing. I mean, I was in the hospital with absolutely nothing to do anyway, so I took advantage of the situation to rest up.

I'd spend three-quarters of the day asleep, and when I did pop my eyes open from time to time like I'd just remembered that I could, I'd see the face of Makoto's mother. Or his father. Or Mitsuru's back.

If it was light outside the window when I woke up, the mother was always right there beside me. A small woman with distinct features, she'd be plopped down in the chair next to the bed, staring at me like she was counting the number of times I blinked. When our eyes met, she'd speak to me briefly, stuff like "How do you feel?" or "Should I turn on the TV?" And that was basically it. She was weirdly hesitant around me, like she was touching something painfully bruised. She acted strange at first, but when I thought about it, it made sense. Makoto had committed suicide, so he must have had the problems to match. She was probably just trying to be considerate.

Mitsuru would always show up later in the afternoon and sit with me for a few hours to give the mother a break. Eternally silent, once he had laid out my supper and then cleaned up after it, he would turn his back to me and pore over all these textbooks and reference books until he left. I learned from the textbooks that he was in twelfth grade.

One day, without thinking too much, I tried to strike up a conversation. "Must be rough getting ready for college entrance exams, huh?"

He shot me a stony glare before he slammed his textbook shut and quickly stepped out into the hallway. Had all that studying messed with his head?

Evening visiting hours were from seven until nine, and Makoto's father never failed to come during this time. A grin would spread across his fleshy face, ear to ear, and instantly, the excessively large private room would be bursting with cheer. Unlike the mother, the father didn't anxiously monitor my face or take particular care in choosing his words. Instead, he went ahead and unburdened himself to me, talking about anything and everything on his mind—"I'm really so happy you came back to life, Makoto" or "I've never thanked God so much before." He was also popular among the nurses, and they often told me what a good father he was. It felt kind of nice, even if he was someone else's father.

Anyway, I got a different impression from each member of this family, but the one thing they seemed to have in common was how deeply they cared about Makoto. I mean, that grumpy brother wouldn't come to the hospital every day if he didn't love him.

For me, they were nothing more than a host family, but for them, Makoto was a son and a brother. The reality of this gradually sank in while I was in the hospital. This might be the one lesson I learned during those sleepy, sluggish, dopey days.

Hospital life ended a week later. I'd fully recovered a while back, but my case was so rare that the hospital was collecting data as it kept an eye on me. (After all, people don't usually come back to life ten minutes after their heart stops.) I was apparently quite the prize, their little miracle boy.

"You did die once there," my still-young doctor told me as he pinched my cheek. "Once is enough, okay? Don't go dying again."

One early Sunday afternoon on a clear autumn day, I was discharged. The whole family came to pick me up, and we all piled into the car and drove to the Kobayashi house in a corner of a quiet residential neighborhood. The spotless living room was filled with flowers in vases, and there was sushi and steak and a whole feast jammed onto a low table in the center. Forgetting how disappointed I'd been a second ago when I saw the very average house, which dashed any remaining hope that they were rich, I was simply moved at the family's warm thoughtfulness. So moved, in fact, that I even gave a little speech on Makoto's behalf. "Thank you so much! All of you!" I'd barely spoken to them while I was in the hospital to keep from slipping up and letting any seams show, so this little display brought hot tears to the corners of his parents' eyes. Talking about full-on familial harmony at its peak here.

Prapura told me how my placement environment would be determined by the size of the mistake I made in my previous life, and if that was the case, I was starting to think that whatever I did, it couldn't have been *that* serious, no big deal. Like maybe I had been a bad drunk. Or a big spender. Or a lady-killer who made women cry.

What I didn't get was why Makoto would go and kill himself when he was blessed with such a loving family. I sometimes forgot that he made the choice to die. The word *suicide* was apparently forbidden in this household since no one even came close to saying it.

"I'll make your favorites for supper, too, Makoto. But maybe you should go lie down for a bit? Have a little nap in your room before supper?" Makoto's mother suggested, kindly, once the table was nearly empty.

I was indeed a bit wiped out by this first taste of happy family life, so this was a welcome proposal. "Yeah. I'll go lie down for a little while."

I stood up and then froze. Even if I wanted to go to Makoto's room, I didn't know where in the house it was. What was I supposed to do now?

"What's wrong, Makoto?" the mother asked.

"You not feeling good?" the father frowned.

The family was getting suspicious. Just then, with impeccable timing, my guide Prapura appeared in the doorway of the living room. Smartly dressed in a suit for some reason, he beckoned for me to follow.

"Okay," I almost said, and then swallowed the word with a gasp. It hit me that I was the only one there who could see the angel.

Prapura climbed the stairs wordlessly, leading his silent charge.

Makoto's bedroom was on the second floor of the house, a Western-style space of about nine square meters. Simple, largely black furniture against a sky-blue rug. The entire room was bright thanks to all the windows, and the fresh green curtains drew in the abundant light. Prapura stopped in front of these curtains, while I sat down on the edge of the bed.

"Been a while, huh?" I said, sardonically. "I figured you'd be teaching me more stuff since you're supposed to be my guide or whatever."

"It's our policy," Prapura replied, smoothly. "Better for you to go in fresh, no preconceived notions. I can't hold your hand every step of the way here. You've gotta get a feel for it yourself."

I stared up at him. Something was off. "Hey, so, you seem totally different from up there?"

"When in Rome, as they say." Prapura gave me a wry grin. "To be honest, I feel like an idiot in all that angel gear on earth. Even if humans can't see me."

"You even sound different, too. You were more polite up there?"

"Clothes make the man, as they say. Ha ha! That was a joke. If I had to say, though, this me's more the real me. We both let our hair down, deal?"

"Uh-huh . . ." What a worldly angel I had on my hands.

"So," Prapura said, his voice suddenly businesslike. "How is your placement so far?"

"Good," I answered, proudly. "Everything's going great. My host family seems nice, and the mom's a good cook. Plus, this room's not so bad. It's way better than I thought it was gonna be. I'm seriously wondering why Makoto Kobayashi would go and kill himself with a life like this."

"That's because," Prapura said, without any expression on his face, "you don't know the truth about your host family yet."

"Huh?"

"You don't know anything." His voice was low and utterly flat, making a shiver run up my spine.

"What's that supposed to mean?"

"However Makoto's father might come off, he's actually painfully self-serving. All that matters to him is that he come out on top. And until very recently, his mother was having an affair with her flamenco instructor. That's what that's supposed to mean."

A burp started to work its way up, and I held it back with effort. I had eaten too much steak at lunch. Now that I was thinking about it, that sushi-steak combo was over the top. Wait, what was Prapura talking about?

"Don't try to run from this. Fine! In that case, I'll give you a bit more detail. Facts that you can't run away from." Prapura glared at me. "Makoto Kobayashi's reasons for committing suicide come together to form a complicated maze. You can't just ride along for free in his body; you have to take on his problems along with it."

The angel's words cut into me mercilessly, plunging me from heaven to hell. Then he sat himself down on the ledge of the bay window, pulled a thick book out of his pocket, and started to flip through it.

"What's that?" I asked.

"The handbook, a must-have for any guide. It contains a record of Makoto Kobayashi's entire life." His hand stopped on one page. "Here we go. A few days before Makoto Kobayashi committed suicide."

I gulped, torn between wanting and not wanting to know at the same time.

"His life was a series of unfortunate events, but this day in particular was the absolute worst. We can assume he had many reasons for wanting to commit suicide, but this day was what set him off," Prapura offered in a slightly pretentious preamble.

The tale he then told solemnly was indeed deserving of the title of "absolute worst day."

"It was September tenth, a Thursday. On his way home from cram school that evening, Makoto Kobayashi witnessed Hiroka Kuwabara walking arm in arm with a middle-aged man."

"Who's Hiroka Kuwabara?"

"An eighth grader at Makoto's school who just happens to be his first love."

"Huh."

"He sees her flirting with this man, and he gets curious, naturally," the angel continued. "So he follows them. And watches as they go into a love hotel."

"Damn!" I gasped.

"This is a huge shock for Makoto. He was literally frozen in place for a minute or two. And then a new tragedy strikes. From the doorway of that very same hotel comes Makoto's mother, snuggling up against her flamenco instructor."

"*That* lady?" That attentive, kind mother? *I* couldn't even believe she'd do something like that. How much more stunned must her actual son have been?

"This night's so awful, it's like a bad joke. And that

wasn't the end of it." Prapura took a deep breath and exhaled slowly. I took a cue from him and did the same to calm my pounding heart. "When Makoto got home, his older brother, Mitsuru, was in front of the TV, his face white as a sheet. He said their father's company had just been on the news. The CEO and several members of the board had been rounded up on suspicion of fraud."

"For real? The father, too?!"

"No, Makoto's father was a rank-and-file employee. He and most of the other employees had nothing to do with the fraud business. It would appear that the CEO, a fairly peculiar man, put together a top-secret development team for the purpose."

"So what'd they do?"

"The indictment is for a mail-order product called Quick'n'Easy Diet Manju. Eating one would take a kilo off, eating two, two kilos. They were selling these steamed buns with this audacious claim. But in reality, the buns were nothing more than your everyday hot-springs *manju*. They were doing all this other nasty stuff, too. The food company was still an up-and-comer. To launch their new octagonal *sembei* crackers, they tried to pass off this malarkey about the earth being octagonal as something remotely plausible. They also took water from the local supermarket taps, slapped the label 'super water' on it, and sold it for a high price . . . They're not so much evil as they are ridiculous."

Prapura shrugged, slightly baffled.

"But, well, be that as it may, they're still Makoto's father's bosses, and he has a responsibility to them. Be it duty or debt, as they say. Anyway, the bosses were all rounded up, and the remaining executives were forced to resign en masse to make up for the whole debacle. So when Mitsuru saw all this on the news, he got worried. Their father was such a sensitive person, he was no doubt deeply upset about the whole thing. And when Makoto heard about it, he got worried, too, of course. However!"

I held my breath for half a second before asking, "There's more?"

"The father finally gets home and he starts to somersault from the door all the way to the living room. He sees Makoto and Mitsuru, throws his arms around them, and kisses them. Then he tries to get them to dance the samba with him."

"Was he drunk?"

"He was. But not the drowning-his-sorrows type of drunk. The good kind of drunk. The celebrating kind. There was a reshuffle at the office after the management's mass exodus, you see. Rank-and-file father found himself suddenly promoted to manager. Three steps up the corporate ladder in one leap. The old man was in high spirits indeed. All 'why the hell would I care if my bosses were arrested or got fired' or what have you. After all, he was finally making his way up in the world, thanks to the scandal," Prapura spat. "Well, maybe that's just how humans are when push comes to shove, but you really don't want to see that side of your own father. The man might have been boring, he might not have stood out in any real way, but Makoto had been proud of his dad and how he kept plugging away. So he was all the more hurt by the whole incident."

I still felt uncomfortably full, my stomach painfully grumbly by the time Prapura finished talking. Perhaps, because the sun was going down, the room that had been so dazzlingly bright earlier was now awfully dark. It felt like the room itself was brooding. To avoid the angel's sharp gaze, I looked up absentmindedly at the ceiling and around at the walls.

There was a mirror on one of them. In it was a reflection of Makoto's face. Narrow eyes. Low flat nose. Compact lips. A deeply nondescript sorry excuse of a face.

When I'd come up against it for the first time in the hospital bathroom, I'd been bitterly disappointed. *Are you telling me to live with a face like this?* I'd cursed Prapura and his boss. Forget about the small details; as a whole, it didn't make anything close to a cheerful impression. A smile did not suit Makoto's face. His eyes had no life in them. At the time, I'd been totally thrown for a loop by this. Why would he look so sad and empty when he had this great family who came to see him every single day? But I felt like I was starting to get it now. His first love going into a love hotel with a middle-aged man. An adulterous mother. A dad who only cared that he was getting his piece of the pie.

"Since we're talking about it, I'll just ask you," I said, glaring at the mirror. "What's the deal with big brother Mitsuru?"

"Since we're talking about it, I'll tell you. He's a callous and malicious young man. He does nothing but harass Makoto. Especially about his height. It bothered Makoto that he was short. The brother knows this and teases him about it on purpose."

"But he hasn't said a thing to me."

"He's ignoring you. He's angry that you'd go and do something so socially unacceptable as suicide. Hey, go on and poke a hand under the bed there."

When I did as I was told, my fingers touched a hard, angular object. I pulled and what came out was a pair of extremely gaudy . . . boots?

"Secret boots," Prapura informed me. "Serious platforms on them. Put those on and you'll suddenly be a lot taller. Makoto doesn't wear them, though. He went and ordered them, but he's a timid thing, so he was afraid people would find out, and he ended up tucking them away under there forever. Mitsuru found them a few days before the suicide. He teased Makoto mercilessly. 'Give up,' he told him. 'Your feet are small, so you're gonna be a shrimp your whole life.' His height, that was the thing that worried Makoto the most."

I tossed the secret boots onto the rug. And then I flopped back on the bed and stared up at the ceiling. All the strength ran out of me. I felt like an idiot for getting caught up in the idea that this was a good family, all love and happiness. What exactly had that little bit of happy home theater over lunch been, then?

"Now I almost can't believe Makoto managed to live this long." I turned a wry smile on Prapura. "A homestay in a place like this, I must've done something seriously awful in my past life."

"Oops! I forgot one thing." The angel wasn't listening to a word I said. "Makoto Kobayashi is currently in ninth grade."

"What?" At this height, I figured he was barely in seventh grade. *Hm? Hang on a second. Ninth grade. That means . . .* I gulped.

"In other words, you've got high school entrance exams in six months," Prapura announced with great delight.

2

What I'd thought was your average happy little family was actually a vipers' nest. On the surface, each of them was kind and loving and warm, but underneath all that, they were hiding seriously nasty truths about who they really were. Nothing but a group of actors going through the motions of being a family. If they were allowed to keep on pretending everything was all sunshine and roses without knowing that the real Makoto was dead, so be it. I figured that meant I could do whatever I wanted.

Standing in the kitchen, the mother looked very much the part of the elegant and stylish housewife in her lovely little lavender apron. Not even the merest shadow of her adultery hanging over her. *Go ahead and keep playing at the good wife and mother if you want. But I'm done with the role of the good son.* I suddenly felt like her home-cooked dinners were tarnished. I started leaving them mostly untouched.

The father. He looked like he'd give up his seat in a heartbeat if an elderly person came along, even in a crowded rush-hour train, and the smile would never leave his face. What did it feel like to sit in his ill-gotten manager's chair, the good fortune that came to him out of his own boss's misfortune? *Go ahead and do your little dance over your teensy promotion with that hypocritical little smile on your face. But don't turn that feeble grin at me.* I stopped answering him when he said goodbye before heading out to work.

Mitsuru, on the other hand, he quickly showed his true face. One morning two days after I was discharged from the hospital, I ran into him in front of the bathroom. I got there a second before he did, so I put my hand on the knob to pull the door open, and he clicked his tongue and said, "Idiot. Can't even manage to die right." He was heartless and malicious, like Prapura said. He'd been ignoring me, so I decided to ignore him back.

Now that I was trying to stay far away from this so-called family, I started locking myself up in Makoto's room. I'd listen to music or the radio, read Makoto's manga, play cards with Prapura at night. I only went downstairs for meals and then quickly scurried back to the room without eating much of anything. I barely moved, so I wasn't hungry anyway. His family didn't so much as raise an eyebrow. Which had to mean that this was the sort of guy Makoto'd been before the suicide.

After a few days of this routine, though, I got pretty bored. On day four, I threw in the towel. I decided it was about time for me to check out Makoto's junior high the following day. Up to that point, I'd been off school to rest up and recover.

The mother didn't say anything, but it looked like she'd secretly been worried about me falling behind. Her eyes shone when I announced that I would be going to school the next day.

I got up early for the first time in forever the next morning and scarfed down a breakfast of an egg-salad-and-tuna sandwich, not leaving a single crumb behind. I brushed my teeth, washed my face with great care, and combed my longish hair. As I stared down my reflection in the bathroom mirror, I thought about how Makoto could be a little less blah if he did something with his hair and his clothes. It's all about what you wear and what you do with your hair, you know. But at the present moment, this boy didn't even look right in his ugly school uniform.

Once I'd gotten ready, I went back to Makoto's room and checked which textbooks I should bring, schedule in one hand. I was so nervous, I'd woken up too early, so I ended up with some time to kill. It didn't take long to set the right textbooks out, and that's when a wave of dread washed over me.

I walked to the window and looked down on the street out front, bright in the morning sun.

Colorful

Students who wore the same uniform as Makoto's were walking in groups past the house.

Two girls holding hands in a friendly way.

A bunch of boys fooling around.

A couple trying to look all grown-up.

I could hear their laughter all the way up here.

I closed the curtains and moved away from the window to sit on the edge of the bed. It was almost time to go, but my body didn't budge. I didn't even bother to answer the mother when she came to call me. I just sat there like a statue until finally Prapura shimmered into existence from behind the bookshelf.

"What the hell are you doing? You're going to be late."

"I'm waiting."

"For what?"

"For someone to come pick me up, obviously."

The instant the words left my mouth, I was overcome by the utter futility of it all.

"Listen," I spat. "Makoto killed himself, but he survived miraculously, and he was in the hospital for a week. When he got out, he was off school for another four days. But no one came to visit. What's that about? No phone calls, no cards, nothing. No one's even come by to bring him his homework or notes or whatever. All of a sudden, I've got a lot of questions about this little situation."

"Unpleasant time for you to notice an unpleasant

thing," Prapura remarked, pulling an unpleasant face. "All right, listen. I'll tell you this right now. Makoto's suicide is not public knowledge. Only his teacher knows. As far as the other students are aware, he had a cold that turned into pneumonia."

"So what if they think it was pneumonia? That doesn't change the fact that no one came to visit." I stared into Prapura's azure eyes, a strange blue with a hint of purple that was impossible to get sick of, the color of the sky right after the sun sets. "Here's the thing. Nothing you tell me could possibly shock me at this point, so I want you to be honest. Did Makoto not have any friends? Was he lonely at school, too?"

The angel's eyes turned the color of the night sky, telling me everything I needed to know.

"Who knows whether or not he was lonely. Only Makoto could answer that question." He sat down next to me, his tone unusually serious. "It's true that he was always alone, but that could also have been because he had his own unique world."

"You mean he was a weirdo?" I asked, frowning.

"There were some students who thought so, yes." Prapura nodded. "Makoto was an introvert and a little on the naïve side. He didn't really talk to his classmates. But really, it was more that he told himself he was that sort of person, y'know? He simply assumed that he was going to be left out, that he'd never be able to get along with anyone. He put up walls and pulled away from people."

"And no one gave him a second glance."

"No, one person did," the angel corrected me. "There was just one kid who'd talk to him without making a big deal of it."

"Who?"

"Hiroka Kuwabara."

His first love . . . I turned my eyes down toward the floor.

"She was the only one who didn't treat Makoto like he was from another planet. She was always cheerful and chatty with him. Maybe she's just one of those people who's like that with everyone, but for Makoto, it was special. Understand? Each and every word she spoke to him meant something."

"And she's in a love hotel with an old man." I flopped back onto the bed. "How's that even work?"

Seriously. A guy this unlucky was really something else. And me, too, backed against the wall and forced to take over for him, I was just as unlucky as Makoto was. This do-over of mine was looking more and more dismal.

"If you're going to hate someone, hate the old you who got you into this. Right now, the main thing is school. If you don't get your butt in gear, you're going to be late." Prapura tried to yank me to my feet.

"I don't want to go to school. I'm done."

"Then you'll be disqualified as Makoto Kobayashi."

"Fine, so I'm disqualified then." I remained fixed to the bed.

"You'll never be able to return to the cycle of rebirth."

"Fine. I don't care."

"I won't play cards with you anymore."

"What—you monster!" I leaped to my feet. My only pleasure in this tedious life was those card games.

"Do you really want to end on a five-loss streak?" He arched a single eyebrow.

"Hngh!" There was no god in this world, only this annoying angel.

A twenty-minute walk to school, Prapura showed me the way, drilling me all the while in all things Makoto. I had to hurry toward the end and slipped through the school gates at a trot. I managed to arrive at Makoto's classroom right before the start of homeroom.

Everyone was already in their seats when I opened the door. They all turned to look at me simultaneously, indescribably strange expressions on their faces. The silence that descended on the room was both an exclamation point and a question mark.

Whatever else was going on, this was clearly not a warm welcome for a classmate returning to school after an extended absence due to illness. I knew right then and there that Prapura hadn't been filling my head with lies about Makoto.

"Woh-kay! Let's get started!" The homeroom teacher came in a few minutes after I took my seat. "We've got a lot of worksheets today. Hand 'em out and get to work. Err, but first, attendance."

Sawada was a thirty-something bachelor who boasted a gorilla-like physique. His superhuman idiocy was apparently also on par with a gorilla. He'd come to visit any number of times while I was in the hospital, but I'd been asleep. This information has been brought to you by Prapura.

"Kobayashi, you here?"

I gasped and saw that all eyes in class had zeroed in on me once more. At the teacher's podium, Sawada had a menacing look on his face. I guess he'd called my name several times already.

"If you're here, say so," he growled.

"Yes, I'm here."

Instantly, the class erupted in frenzied whispers.

Even Sawada's eyes widened in surprise.

"Oh, Kobayashi. You sound pretty cheerful today," he noted.

Whoa, hey there. This is how I always sound.

Keeping this thought to myself, I spoke again just to

see how everyone would react. "Yes. Thanks to all of you, I'm fully recovered."

The cacophony of whispers doubled in volume.

Apparently, the strangest thing in their world was a cheerful, enthusiastic Makoto. People gawked at me for the rest of that day, like they were about to witness an alien give birth. They all seemed to find me unsettling.

But of course, they were simply surprised that Makoto had changed; no one suspected he had a new soul. So no matter how shocked people were or how high they raised their eyebrows, I was going to pay absolutely zero attention to them and do whatever I pleased. I mean, however weird whatever I did seemed, as long as I was wearing the body of Makoto Kobayashi, that made me plenty Makoto Kobayashi.

This was the general rule I'd decided to live by, but there was at least one person at that school with unbelievably sharp eyes.

It happened on lunch break and nearly gave me a heart attack. I was heading back to class after a nap behind a tree in the rear courtyard when suddenly I heard someone trotting after me in the hallway. I looked back to find a tiny girl with hair in a neat bob staring up at me intently. If she was tiny from Makoto's perspective, then she had to have been pretty small.

"Seminar?" the shrimp said, abruptly, her shiny eyeballs

bulging. "C'mon. You went to a seminar, right? You went and discovered a new you, right?"

"What?" I was baffled.

"Don't you try to fool me. I can tell." She narrowed her eyes. "You've been acting strange all day. You're not the usual Kobayashi."

"What are you on about?" I flinched and took a step back.

"I knew it." She looked extremely smug. "I just knew it. I saw an article about that seminar before. You pay a ton of money and they brainwash you. You get reborn as a better you. Am I right? I'm right, aren't I? You skipped school to go to this seminar. And you were reborn into an optimistic, positive, cheerful human being. But I don't think it suits you at all."

"Excuse me?" Now I was annoyed. "I'll tell you right now. I didn't go to any seminar."

"So then what? What else is there?"

"I didn't do anything."

"Liar. I don't believe you."

"Fine. Don't believe me."

What was this girl's problem? And what about me was so optimistic or positive or cheerful? Although I still had questions, I started to walk away from her. Better not to get too deep with these types.

"I totally don't believe you!" she howled, stubbornly,

right before I turned the corner. "I can tell. You definitely did something. You might be able to fool everyone else, but you're not fooling me!"

Tiny weirdo. But strangely sharp.

I kept my cool, but I was pretty shaken up. I raced to a stall in the boys' bathroom and called Prapura.

"Who the heck was that?"

"The thing is, well . . ." He already had the handbook open when he appeared before me. But there was no trace of his usual bravado. The fingers that flipped the pages moved with a slight hint of uncertain impatience.

"Nothing." He finally gave up and closed the book. "She's not in here."

"What do you mean, she's not in there?"

"The fact that she's not in the handbook means, in other words, that the girl didn't exist in Makoto's memories."

"So then, basically," I said, "he didn't notice her?"

"Well." Prapura nodded. "In a word, yes."

"Huh." As I gave the useless handbook the side eye, a mix of complicated emotion welled up in me.

A weirdo shrimp who even Makoto Kobayashi hadn't noticed. And she was the only one who had sniffed out that I wasn't Makoto.

The first day back felt like forever. In the classroom, everyone attacked me with their eyes, and in the hallway, I was accosted by that shrimp. I was utterly wiped out by the time the last homeroom was over. But despite that, after school, I wanted to take a peek at just one more place.

The art room.

Prapura had told me only that very morning that Makoto had been quite the passionate member of the school art club. As far as I could tell, this guy hadn't had a single thing going for him, but it turned out he'd been a master painter. He basically kept attending school only so that he could go to art class and art club.

Makoto had continued going to the club even in the second term, despite the fact that the general rule was to quit any extracurricular activities at the end of the first term in ninth grade. Still, there were other ninth graders who went, and the club advisor not only tolerated it, but actively encouraged this passion Makoto and the others had for art.

I didn't think Makoto's passion had been directed solely at the canvas, though.

Once classes were over, I went up to the art room on the third floor of the new school building and looked for Makoto's canvas on the shelf at the back. I found a half-finished oil painting there, so I laid out the oil paints and set the canvas on an easel. I could've just left it at that, but once I set everything up, I found myself wanting to paint.

I sat down on a folding chair and faced Makoto's

canvas for ten minutes. Finally, I squeezed some paint onto the wooden palette and got to work on the unfinished picture. At first I was merely copying what was already on the canvas, but then my brush gradually took on a life of its own, and before I knew it, I was frolicking in the world of the painting.

The brick-colored light of the afternoon sun poured into the warm classroom, while the scent of oil paints that tickled my nose comforted me. In this rich silence, I could feel Makoto there with me. There were a dozen or so other people in the room, but they were also focused on their canvases, their faces intent with passionate concentration. No one was staring at me like in Grade Nine Class A. And the occasional bit of quiet banter or laughter made the room even more agreeable to me.

Here, in this art room, Makoto was able to relax.

In the place alone, he could be himself.

When I realized why he came here, my chest tightened inexplicably.

At the same moment, I heard a voice like a bittersweet fruit. "Haven't seen you in a while, Makoto."

I knew who it belonged to before I even turned around. Hiroka Kuwabara. I'd come here because I wanted to catch a glimpse of her.

Flustered, I looked back to find a pleasingly chubby girl with brown hair peeking at Makoto's canvas.

Colorful

"Where were you, Makoto? You didn't show up to the club at all. I was so worried you'd never finish this painting. This is, like, my fave. You know, I come just to see your painting. Aah, okay. I'm kidding, but still."

Prapura'd already told me that this wasn't true. Hiroka Kuwabara didn't do any extracurricular activities, but a good friend of hers was in the art club, so she'd come hang out sometimes whenever the whim took her. And Makoto would always, always wait with bated breath for the moment she came and talked to him in her little baby voice.

"I'm so glad you're all better. I soooo want you to finish this painting. Your stuff's been so super dark lately, Makoto. But I've been hoping this one'll be happy, like, the first colorful painting you've done in forever."

This girl who crouched down to talk to me, the girl who was practically pressing her cheek against mine, was very different from how I'd pictured Hiroka Kuwabara. I thought she'd be more mature, acting like she was too cool for school, but her voice and her way of speaking were both extremely childish. Even so, she was weirdly sexy. Each time her long hair touched her cheeks, my heart threatened to leap out of my chest. Of course, that was just Makoto's body responding to her.

"You can't skip anymore." She waggled a finger in front of my face. "You have to promise Hiroka. I, Makoto Kobayashi, promise Hiroka Kuwabara to finish this beautiful painting, pinky promise? I mean, this horsey here, it's crying. Wah-wah, so sad, I'm only half-finished."

Even though Hiroka was in eighth grade, younger than Makoto, she didn't call him by his last name in the usual show of respect. She called him Makoto. Makoto had no doubt been totally blown away by this kind of adorable endearment.

"So, look, this horsey, you did, like, a super great job here. I know it's still only an outline, but I can hear it breathe, y'know? Flying through the sky, right? So cool."

She wasn't beautiful, but she was strangely coquettish. Her soft, milky pale skin made me shiver. Maybe it was because I couldn't shake off the image of her at a love hotel, but just thinking about how I could reach out and touch those plump lips made my lower half go numb. Aah, again, of course, Makoto's lower half just went ahead and . . .

"The blue in the background's, like, super pretty, too. You don't really see this kind of blue, huh? It's so vast an' clear, like this big ol' empty sky. I've never seen a sky like this before, okay? But I love it."

The best part about Hiroka Kuwabara was that she would just talk and talk whether or not Makoto said anything in reply. This had to have been such a huge relief for Makoto, who hadn't been such a great talker.

But I couldn't actually bring myself to agree with what

she was saying. The blue spread across the canvas, and the horse floated up on the top right, still half-finished. The horse didn't look like much of anything, to be honest. It looked more like the blue was the main part of the painting, and Hiroka was saying it was the sky. But I actually . . .

"I think it's the ocean."

I heard a familiar voice from behind me, and my heart skipped a beat. I'd been thinking the same thing.

"A horse flying through the sky would be great, too, but to me, this definitely looks like the horse is swimming in the ocean. It's at the bottom of a deep, quiet sea, and it's slowly heading toward the surface of the water. Look, see? The blue up here is a little brighter, right?"

"That's exactly it!" I looked back at the owner of the voice, eagerly. And all my excitement instantly vanished.

"See? I told you." The shrimp grinned with self-satisfaction. "You can't fool these eyes of mine."

3

Her name was Shoko Sano. I found out she was in the same class as Makoto—Grade Nine Class A—and on top of that, she also belonged to the art club. And yet Makoto somehow never even saw her. Well, maybe it was just that all Makoto ever saw was Hiroka Kuwabara. At any rate, from then on, I was plagued by this Shoko Sano.

She was utterly convinced that Makoto was not the real Makoto (and you know, she was right on the mark there), and she was incredibly persistent, constantly underfoot, as if she were trying to rip off the monster's mask.

"If it wasn't a seminar, then maybe hypnosis?"

"There's no way . . . I mean, I feel like there's no way, but just be honest and tell me the truth, okay? Did you get exorcised of demons in Sri Lanka?"

"Got it! You went swimming with dolphins?"

"This guy my dad knows, okay? He turned into this totally different person the second his baby was born. But I mean, you couldn't possibly have had a baby at your age, Kobayashi."

She came at me with one new theory after another. I had no idea where on earth she was getting all these wild ideas from.

"I don't believe in hypnosis."

"Exorcising demons? If I was going to do that, I'd ask an angel."

"I'm a terrible swimmer."

"I have no recollection of it, but I would use birth control."

At first, I refuted each one in turn, but it gradually got to be too much of a hassle and pointless in the end, anyway. So I started to run away the second I so much as sensed her presence. The safest place of refuge turned out to be the art room. Strangely, the only time she didn't bother me was when I was painting. She never failed to stay back a fixed distance, quietly peering at my canvas from behind. I guess for someone into art, this room was a kind of sacred space.

Embarrassing confession here but, yes, I kept going to art club even after that. What can I say? I had nothing else to do, and I couldn't bring myself to go straight home. Staying late after school was a hundred times better than getting all annoyed having to deal with that family.

I was also curious about Hiroka Kuwabara. Long story short, like Makoto, I started to hold my breath and wait for her to come over and talk to me. I was completely aware that this was not the greatest of ideas—I knew she was one of the people who had made Makoto suffer. Even so, Hiroka had an appeal that was hard to pin down. I wanted her to shower me with her senseless babbling in her baby voice. She even made me daydream about being the man she'd been with that night instead.

Still, the main reason I was always in the art room was simply that I'd come to appreciate the pure pleasure of painting. I intended to take my time finishing Makoto's blue picture. Maybe because my physical body had indeed belonged to him, I quickly grew accustomed to the oil paints and my skill grew by leaps and bounds. It wasn't so much that I was acquiring the techniques; it felt more like gradually getting back a thing that had always belonged to me.

Put the brush to the canvas carefully.

And then a little something was born, something that hadn't existed a second ago.

As I repeated this one step, the little something turned into a big something.

Soon, the something began to form a vague world.

It was my world.

Mine and Makoto's.

Only when I sank into the world of the painting did I forget Makoto's misfortunes, his life, his loneliness, his misery, and his height. With each passing day, I grew more entranced by the oils. The second-term midterm exams were fast approaching, but I still faithfully kept going to the art room after school, even when no one else did.

Which led to my homeroom teacher, Mr. Sawada, calling me into his office right after exams were over.

"Listen, Kobayashi. I know you were absent for a while there, all right? Must've been a rough time mentally, too. But even taking that into consideration . . ." Sawada waved the list of exam results. "This is beyond awful."

I couldn't have agreed more.

After school in the gloomy teachers' room, Sawada and I sat together with huge headaches over the very serious issues Makoto faced at the moment. His academic performance was outstandingly poor; his average in the three core subjects of Japanese, math, and English on the midterm exams had been 35 percent, and that dropped to 31 percent when the rest of the term's subjects were added in.

"Aah, well, sure." Sawada shrugged. "You could say this is consistent with the grades you were getting in the first term. But, listen. Ninth graders normally start to panic by the time they get to the second term. Are you aware that high school exams are coming up? If you keep noodling along like this you won't have a chance." His thick eyebrows hung low on his face. Sawada was deeply troubled.

I, too, was deeply troubled.

At the end of the day, these were Makoto Kobayashi's exams. They were testing him on all the things he should have already learned before I took the wheel. So even if I barely paid attention in class, I was sure that once I opened the exam booklet, Makoto's brain cells would just take over from there and do their thing. But when I did actually have the booklet in front of me, I'd had this faint sense of dread sink into the pit of my stomach. I couldn't believe his brain cells were *this* useless.

"This here?" Sawada rapped a sharp finger on the paper in front of him. "You're in real danger of not getting into high school at all."

'Twas the season and all, so the conversation gradually turned in the direction of the entrance exams.

According to Sawada, what really counted when it came to getting into high school was everything up to the second term of ninth grade. It wasn't just your exam results they looked at. There was apparently this sort of synthesized score that meshed together stuff like your attitude in class, your attendance, and the number of reports and essays you submitted. Makoto had gotten basically the worst score in the first term. Sawada didn't come right out and say it, but I got the sense that "worst" here was exactly what it sounded like, the lowest of everyone in the class.

Colorful

All of which meant his back was to the wall. Makoto had to do whatever it took to turn things around in the second half of the term.

"That's where we're at here." Sawada shook his head, almost hopelessly. "So what's it going to be, Kobayashi? Keep this up, and your only shot's going to be focusing on a single private school."

"A single private school?"

"If you really buckle down and study like your life depends on it, we're looking at a different story. Then we might have a hope of you pulling off a decent score on the entrance exam itself. But it's risky to bet the farm on the exam when you've got this synthesized score hanging around your neck. You want a rock solid way forward; you're looking at applying to just one school with a referral. I know requirements for referrals have gotten looser at public schools lately, but still, your best bet's to apply for early decision to just one private school."

"So even *I* could make it if I focus on applying to just one school?"

He nodded. "If you don't care what school it is."

Just one school. I didn't understand much of this, but I decided right then and there that that's what I'd do.

"Okay, that sounds good."

"What?"

"I've decided to just apply to one private school."

45

"Decided? Look, don't make up your mind right away—"

"I don't care what high school I go to."

"But the level you're at now could only get you into . . ."

"It's fine," I declared. "I'm fine with my level."

I figured that was the end of the conversation, so I stood up from my chair. I guess there wasn't anything to get worked up about here.

"So you're the coasting type, huh?" Sawada cocked his head to one side. He lowered his voice so that none of the other teachers would hear him. "Lot of you lately. Applying to high school with basically zero drive. No fighting spirit. Well, sure. Why not? But you still got some time. I want you to really think it over. And talk to your parents about this."

He grabbed my shoulder with his meaty hand and pushed me back into the chair. "How've you been anyway? You know."

"Know what?"

"You know, that, um, you know. The, uh . . ." Sawada mumbled, awkwardly. "Ah, you know, that whole thing. Your mom asked me not to mention it for a while, but I'm just . . . concerned, you know?"

"Ohh." I suddenly understood what he was getting at. "You mean the suicide?"

"H-hey," he hissed. "You don't just *say* it."

"Well, if that's what you're talking about, I'm fine now.

I wasn't thinking straight. I won't do it again." I gave him a very "everything's all right" smile.

Sawada leaned in close. "You sure?"

"I'm sure."

"You wanna bet on it?"

"I won't bet on it."

"Stingy."

"I could say the same about you, Mr. Sawada."

"Yeah, I do feel like you've had some kind of break-through lately." He stared at me hard, his gorilla face firm. "But you tell me right away if you run into any trouble in class or anything. I'll help. You know my help's amaaaaazing."

This was apparently no lie. According to Prapura, Sawada really had a way with his students and worked to keep them safe. He was always saying, "I catch you bullying anyone, I'll knock you into next week. *Then* I'll hear what you have to say." Getting this man as his homeroom teacher was maybe one of the few—near-zero—bits of good luck Makoto had had.

Lost in thought, I bowed to him lightly and left the teachers' room.

That night, I announced to Makoto's mother, "I'm going to focus on a single private high school. Just one entrance exam."

Personally, I was just hoping to put the issue of cram school to bed. Makoto hadn't attended since his suicide, and I wanted to quit. As long as I didn't have any lofty aspirations, I'd manage to get into high school with whatever academic abilities I happened to have now. "What? Really? You already decided?" She seemed upset by my sudden declaration. "Did you discuss this with your teacher?"

"Yeah."

"And he said this is what you should do?"

"Mm."

"I see . . ." She fell into deep thought.

I, too, was preoccupied with something other than her reaction to my big news. It was seven p.m., the time we usually had supper. And yet this evening, the only people around the living room table were the mother and me. Why was it so quiet?

Mitsuru was one thing, since he went to cram school pretty much every night. But this was the first time since I'd gotten out of the hospital that the father wasn't sitting here like a lump.

"Dad's going to go back to working overtime again." The mother turned her eyes toward the father's empty seat, as if seeing the unspoken question written on my face. "I'm sure you understand, Makoto. The company's going through some tough times right now. They're really having to work to get back the public trust after the corruption scandal. Dad insisted that you were more important, though, and arranged it so he could come home early for the last while. But it's getting a bit tricky for him to keep doing that. You're doing pretty well now, so he decided to roll up his sleeves and get back to work."

"Huh." I snorted. "Must be rough being the manager."

"It is." She nodded, serious. Too dense to catch the sarcasm, apparently. "He has a lot of new things to learn."

Did this mean supper was basically going to be me and her from now on? The mere thought of it depressed me. I mean, any kid was going to be put off by the idea of having dinner alone with his mom, and it wasn't even *my* mother here. A depraved old lady, a total stranger. A married adulteress. None of this actually had anything to do with me, but still, a visceral discomfort with the whole mess sort of exploded up from the pit of my stomach sometimes and made me horribly cruel.

"Y'know, eating supper just the two of us?" Yup, like this, for example. I shot a look of laser-focused contempt at the mother's nervous eyes. "I dunno. Makes me wanna vomit." I dropped my chopsticks and returned to my room on quick feet.

After that, her eyes would be red and teary whenever I passed by her going to the bathroom or something, and it did make me feel bad in a way. But she was the one in the wrong in the first place. Why should I get stuck with these twitchy pangs of conscience? So then I would get twice as angry. I despised these tears of hers, I was sure they were just for show.

They were nothing more than a simple host family, just a temporary place to rest my head, and yet I was always on edge in the Kobayashi house. At times like this, I would think about Hiroka Kuwabara, a soothing magic to calm my raging heart.

Her round face, her syrupy voice cast a spell, comforting me. I spent more and more of each passing day daydreaming about her, although I still didn't know if it was what you'd call love. Sometimes, on sleepless nights, I'd even fantasize about her while I satisfied the needs of Makoto's body. This guy was annoyingly high maintenance.

After spending a number of days like this, I started to have doubts about the memories in Prapura's guidebook. Simply put, I started to feel like the whole thing was a misunderstanding on Makoto's part.

The way I saw it, the middle-aged man with Hiroka must have been her father. Makoto had just jumped to the wrong conclusion, like how people always did on TV or in manga. He'd fallen into the most common of traps. Of course. That was obviously what happened . . . But then why a love hotel, of all places?

Oh! Her father collapsed! Yes, right. He was walking around with Hiroka and he suddenly got very sick. Hiroka looked around for a place where he could lie down, but there was nowhere. She had no other choice but to rent a love hotel room for two hours so he could rest. Happens all the time. I've seen it happen myself. You could even say it's an everyday occurrence—as if.

As if. No way.

"Um, I wanted to ask you something." I turned to Prapura one night, too tangled up in my own thoughts to come to any real answers about anything. "So I'm in the body of Makoto Kobayashi, but I'm really just a soul, right? A soul, that's a spirit. It's light and invisible and can basically fly all free wherever it wants, right?"

"If," Prapura replied, curtly. "If you wanted to fly 'all free' to Hiroka Kuwabara's room and peep while she changes, you'd best abandon that idea immediately."

"Eep!" I was taken aback. "How'd you know?"

"Men always ask me that." The angel's voice was cold; he was apparently sick of this line of questioning. "Every Tom, Dick, and Harry thinks a soul is a ghost or an invisible man. They just lump them all together into the same box. But I am sorry to inform you that you are not free like a ghost, and you don't have any special talents like invisibility. You're nothing more than a soul without a shell. Plus, you're bound to Makoto Kobayashi's flesh now, so you can't come and go as you please. If you absolutely must see Hiroka Kuwabara changing, you'll have to go in through the front door like everyone else."

"Hngh!" I threw myself back on the bed, crestfallen.

"Hey!" Prapura snapped, his voice even colder now. "You didn't actually call me here just to discuss your baser instincts, did you?"

Pouting, I sat up and looked at the angel by the window. He was wearing his usual poker face, but his eyes were as cold as his voice. He looked upset.

I leaped off the bed and pulled the cards of out my desk drawer. "How about we go for round seven?" I grinned up at him.

Prapura pointed to the desk chair without returning my smile. "Sit a minute."

"Huh?"

"Just sit."

"Uh-huh." At an impasse, I sat.

"Now, look." Prapura was on me immediately, lecturing me with enough force to strip the guts out of my body, like he was cleaning a fish he'd just pulled out of the water. "I've wanted to ask you this for a while now, but are you— how can I put this—are you aware of the fact that you're here for a do-over? You do know that this is a place for you to find new discipline and get stronger, yes? If I didn't actually stand up and say something, how long would you drift along like this?"

Colorful

It'd been about a month since the start of my homestay. And apparently, Prapura was not pleased with my way of being Makoto Kobayashi.

"Given that this is a do-over, a certain amount of do-ing is indeed required here," he said, his tone unusually severe.

I'd failed in my previous life in this world, and now I was supposed to somehow work my soul hard enough that it reached the level where I qualified for rebirth once again. With verve! Gusto! Guts! And yet here I was, with-out even a single one of those exclamation points attached to any of my actions. Although Prapura thought highly of my enthusiasm for oil painting, I wasn't doing anything *but* oil painting, and the only thing in my head was Hiroka Kuwabara. And now that I'd defaulted to the easiest op-tion for the entrance exams, it was clear that there wasn't much in the way of discipline or training happening in this life of mine. But if I didn't train, my soul would be stuck at the same level. And I could only remember the mistake I'd made in my past life when my soul leveled up. As long as I continued along this path, Prapura doubted that would ever happen.

"I mean, you're not even *trying* to recall your past life, are you? Have you forgotten what you're here for? Believe me, it gives me no pleasure to sit you down like this, but being a guide starts to feel pretty meaningless when the person you're supposed to be guiding doesn't even make half an effort. Honestly. I'm jealous of the guides with souls who actually show up." Prapura ended his lecture with this complaint, and then sighed as he sat down on the edge of the bed.

"You done?" I asked, but I got no reply. He was apparently done. "Okay then, just let me say this. I *have* thought about this mistake in my past life. Like, I must've screwed up pretty bad to end up in a placement like this. Maybe I killed someone. Maybe I stole a whole bunch of money. Maybe a hundred people got hurt because I messed up. But do you think it's fun to think about that stuff? It's a bummer. It's seriously depressing."

I crossed my legs and sat up straighter as I glared at him, resentfully.

"First of all, okay? Even if I did somehow remember this mistake of mine and manage to say farewell to this body, it'll just be some other sucker next time. Say I'm reborn as—I dunno—Jun Komori or Shin Koyama, I've got no guarantee they'll be any better than Makoto Kobayashi. I honestly doubt the next go-round's for sure going to be a life of sunshine and roses, you know?"

"Or Yuko Koike or Yoko Kogawa, hm?" Prapura added, with a serious look. "You won't necessarily be reborn as a man."

"The thing here is that *I* might be different when I'm

reborn, but the world I'm born into won't. Maybe I'll end up facing the same terrible situation in my next life that I did in my previous life. All the stuff that happened to Makoto Kobayashi could happen to Jun Komori or Yoko Koike, too."

"In other words, the fact that the conditions are the same for everyone. No one is born with any sort of guarantee."

"Just like a homestay placement, right? Hit or miss. You won't know until you open the box." I laughed, coldly. "Your boss sure likes the hard sell."

Although I was just arguing for the sake of arguing at first, the more I talked, the more I felt sad for real. I was actually a lot more scared and anxious than I'd realized about all of this, about being born into some other strange family, about having to start life over from scratch and form new relationships in that new world.

Honestly. What had my past life been like?

Prapura placed a hand on my shoulder. I looked back with a wry smile and he returned it as he reached out toward the desk. His fingers wrapped around the cards. "How about it? Round seven?"

A do-over was so easy in a game.

4

The first Sunday in November, I cut Makoto's mop of hair and pushed up the front with some hair mousse.

When I passed Hiroka in the hallway at school the next day, she cried out, "Makoto, you look so hot!" This compliment was the finest moment of my Makoto Kobayashi life.

I withdrew Makoto's savings and bought some popular sneakers, and soon, all the guys in class were whispering in my ear. "Wow. How much did those cost?"

When I talked to the guys sitting near me these days, like "When's the next gym period?" or "Lend me an eraser," they didn't jump like I was a pregnant alien anymore. My classmates were gradually getting used to my version of Makoto Kobayashi. All except for Shoko Sano, who continued to doggedly investigate the mystery of my transformation.

I was also making good headway—albeit slowly—on my work in progress. I had a real chance of finishing the whole painting before school let out for winter break.

Colorful

Prapura had given me that big lecture about training, but now that I really thought about it, I was indeed making progress, just doing it in my own way, at my own pace. I still had zero interest in training to be reborn, but I could at least be a little creative and make my life as Makoto more comfortable. See how it makes me look taller with my bangs spiked up with the mousse?

"Don't let your guard down." Prapura wagged a finger at me just when I was feeling a bit proud of myself, like I was finally getting the hang of this. "A homestay's like driving a car. It's most dangerous when you start to get used to it."

He was exactly right.

Bad stuff has this way of just attacking out of the blue. It's actually there all the time, though, carefully laying in wait on all sides, just out of sight.

Once I settled on a policy of "happily attending whatever high school would have me," I put the entrance exams completely out of my head. I assumed everyone else had done the same. So when the father asked that I go to a public high school instead, one night in the middle of November when he joined us for supper for the first time in two weeks, it was a total bolt from the blue.

Why now?! I didn't see the plot twist coming at all.

"Truth is, Mitsuru's switched his major for college. He

wants to go into medicine now." The father tentatively broached the subject, looking extremely uncomfortable, as we faced each other over the heated *kotatsu* table that had recently appeared in the Kobayashi living room. "He's been studying for the entrance exam every day morning till night. He's really putting his heart into it, giving it everything he has. Your mom and I'd like to make that dream happen for him, but you know, the tuition for medical school is outrageously expensive, even for public ones. If we're paying for your private school tuition on top of that, well, to be honest, for this family, it's a little . . ." He trailed off, and the mother picked up where he left off.

"You know your dad's company's going through a rough patch right now. They're still sorting everything out. The senior management's all been replaced. And the company hasn't managed to get their clients' trust back yet. Dad *did* get promoted, but he might not get his bonus this year. And we don't know what's going to happen from now on, either." She rambled on and on before pulling up abruptly. "Oh! But of course, this is just if you can get into a public school. Obviously, if you don't pass the exam, that would be the end of that."

"But Makoto." The father picked up the baton. "Why don't you give it a go at least? You do the best you can, and we'll manage the rest somehow. I'd like to see you get in the ring and really fight for something."

Whoa, whoa. Here we go with the fighting again. Fight. Fight. Why did this word make me feel so lifeless?

"Well, I'll think about it," I said, and hurried back to my room.

Give the public school exam a go . . .

I flopped down on the bed and stared up at the ivory ceiling. It wasn't like I desperately wanted to go to any particular private school, unlike Mitsuru with his clear goal of medicine. If there wasn't the money for it, then I figured I was basically stuck with sitting for the public school exam. The real issue was how long I'd be doing this homestay anyway. What if I studied my butt off only to say goodbye to Makoto's body before I got to go to the school I'd worked so hard to get into? The mere thought of it sank me to the bottom of a gloomy pit.

"Makoto, do you have a moment ? I'm coming in," I heard the mother say from the bottom of my pit. Without waiting for an answer, she opened the door and came waltzing right in. "Sorry for bringing the entrance exams up out of nowhere like this."

I had hurriedly dived under my duvet and felt her come to a stop somewhere near my feet.

"But this is something we've really thought long and hard about. Your dad and I've discussed it a bunch of times. And we even asked your teacher Mr. Sawada for his opinion."

"Sawada?" Why was she bringing up Sawada?

"We wanted to consider every possibility. We were worried this might push you up against the edge again."

The mother sounded unusually tense, and it finally clicked. Makoto had only just come back from the brink of death, and they didn't know why he'd tried to kill himself. She was afraid it might have been because he'd been worried about the high school entrance exam.

"But I had a hunch. No matter what kind of problems you have, studying's the one thing you're not too concerned about." Her voice softened slightly. "After all, you've never cared about your grades, not a whit, not since you were little. It never mattered to you if you got a great score on a test or if you failed it. And your class ranking's never bothered you. You've always hated competing, haven't you? At field day at school, you always looked a little sad, whether you won or lost the race. The only time you were honestly happy about winning was when you were playing cards. You're just like that. So I knew it wasn't your studies that was weighing on you. Of course, I couldn't say for sure, one hundred percent, but Mr. Sawada told me, too, it's the overachievers who end up snapping before entrance exams."

As I listened to her, I felt this warm closeness toward Makoto. Maybe he'd also hated the word *fight*. The sweat, the tears, the victory! The idea that you had no choice but to push yourself, go above and beyond in some match you didn't even care about.

"It's fine. I'll take the public school exam. For your information, I didn't try to kill myself because of entrance exams or anything." I sat up, still hidden under the duvet. "You should look to your own heart if you want to know why I tried to commit suicide." I always ended up running my mouth off when I saw the mother.

"What do you mean?" Her face clouded over.

"I told you. Ask your own self."

"I can't know unless you tell me."

"Then think about it until you figure it out."

"I've thought about it. I can't *stop* thinking about it!" Her shadow suddenly twisted across the rug. "Makoto. Please. Talk to me. You don't have to carry this all by yourself. Your dad said we should wait until you came to us and opened up on your own, but I just can't wait anymore. Please. Tell me what happened. What was so hard for you? What was so bad you wanted to die? What happened? I'm going to have a nervous breakdown myself if we keep not talking about it!" she yelled hysterically.

Those dark circles under her eyes, she acts like she's the victim here, I thought, and I lost it. "Okay. Then I'll tell you."

Stop! I heard Prapura roar angrily in my head, but I couldn't pull back now.

"How's your flamenco teacher doing?" I looked up at her and grinned.

Like a frost falling on a winter night, her face froze, eyelids first, then cheeks, lips—all trace of movement stopped. Her eyes alone darted about. This was the reaction of someone who was painfully aware of exactly what I was talking about.

I knew it. I got to my feet and slipped past her to dig into my closet. I yanked on the black hoodie Makoto's savings had paid for and made for the front door, wallet in one hand. I looked back as I was about to leave the room and saw her bent over crying, her shoulders shaking.

It was raining when I stepped outside. The droplets that hit my cheeks were cold enough to make me shiver. Now that I thought about it, I'd been feeling a little feverish since that morning, like I was coming down with a cold or something. But I kept on walking, umbrella in one hand.

The moonless and starless November night looked pathetic somehow, like the boss up there had made a mistake.

"You're the pathetic one." Prapura abruptly popped into existence next to me. He was brandishing a frilly white parasol that totally did not go with his classy trench coat.

Of course this is what angels are into.

"Distributed by the boss. I would never buy an umbrella

like this myself," Prapura said, glaring at me. "At any rate, I'm more interested in what you're trying to do here. Is it your intent to destroy Makoto's family?"

"I'm just saying what Makoto couldn't before he died," I replied. I was honestly fed up with all of this shit. "The more I find out about him, the clearer it is to me that he was lost, he was so unlucky. He was shy and quiet, and then he died without saying a word to anyone. But I'm different. I'm sure I was a serial killer, or a robber, or a total piece of garbage in my past life. If that's what I was, I've got nothing to lose now. I'm going to do all the things Makoto couldn't."

"Ooh-hoo, amazing. So you're a superhero now." Prapura whistled, but all the while, his eyes on me were harsh. "However, are you really doing this for Makoto's sake? Or is it actually all for yourself? After all, you find Makoto dull and unappealing, you don't like his family. Nothing's going the way you want, and now you're being forced to actually study for the entrance exams. You're angry. You're taking it out on his mother. And now you're standing here telling me it's all for Makoto?"

"Shut up!" I threw my umbrella to the ground and walked faster.

"Wait! Hey!" Prapura scooped my umbrella up and came after me. "All I'm saying is not to jump to conclusions, okay? The Makoto everyone says was so shy and quiet might not have been the real Makoto. Maybe they all went and decided that without really knowing him at all, who knows. Maybe they just pushed him into that box, forced him to wear that label. The same thing applies to you, whether you were a serial killer and all that in your past life, you shouldn't rush to conclusions. There are all kinds of mistakes, after all."

My head felt like lead and throbbed with pain. Prapura might as well have been speaking Greek for all the sense he was making to me right now. I kept walking, silent.

"Hey! Where are you going?" he shouted after me.

"What's it to you?"

"You don't even know where you're going."

"Leave me alone."

"Listen, you need to go home."

"You go home. Back up there."

"I have a duty as your guide."

"So then guide me." I stopped in my tracks. "Guide me to Hiroka Kuwabara."

Once I had this amazing idea, my headache conveniently went away. "Seriously. I'm begging you. I really need to see her face. I want to hear her voice. I won't ask you to show me her changing or anything like that."

Prapura looked thoughtful and not particularly inclined to do me any favors.

"I don't mind guiding you," he said, finally, pity in his

eyes. "But if you see her tonight, you'll only end up hurt—a little at the very least."

"Hurt?"

"Like Makoto Kobayashi was."

"Oh."

The night got about five degrees colder as I guessed at what Prapura meant. I felt like I was suffocating, like a hand of ice had my heart in its grip. Maybe there was no way for me to escape the fate that bound Makoto. But even still . . .

"Even still, I'm not like Makoto." I took a deep breath. "I'm not as weak as he was."

Prapura's face was shadowed gray beneath the black and white umbrellas.

I snatched the black one from his hand and marched ahead. "Let's go."

I wanted to know the truth about Hiroka Kuwabara, however awful and painful.

5

Get on a bus at the nearby stop, ride it for twenty minutes. Walk ten minutes from the station where it finishes its trip. A small café called Lullaby stands in one corner of an obscenely neon-lit backstreet. After Prapura told me that that's where I'd find Hiroka Kuwabara, I went on the hunt, doubtful that a place with a name this outdated even existed in this day and age. But I found it surprisingly quickly.

Hiroka was walking out the door when I came across the café sign around nine p.m. I saw a bluish shadow on the other side of the purple glass of the automatic door, and then it slid aside to reveal her wearing a dark green jacket and looking very grown-up. Behind her was a middle-aged man, maybe in his forties or fifties. At a glance, he looked like your average businessman, in the usual crisp suit and tie. The corners of his eyes turned downward the same way Hiroka's did. So maybe he really was her dad.

It was ludicrous that I was still thinking like this at this stage of the game, and as if to strike the final blow and banish all illusion from my heart, Hiroka and the old man stepped into the narrow alley and headed toward an even more suspiciously secluded area.

I followed them, hiding my face with my umbrella. Just like Makoto had gone after them a few days before his suicide. And then, just like that night, they stopped in front of a love hotel. European-themed with white walls. At first glance, it looked like any other hotel in the city center.

The man seemed perfectly healthy, full of energy like he was raring to go, and sadly looked nothing like a dad feeling poorly. He had an arm wrapped around Hiroka's shoulders and was casually leading her toward the hotel entrance.

I didn't want to just stand there in shock like Makoto had, so I took a deep breath and stepped forward. The man walked into the hotel first, leaving Hiroka to fold up her umbrella in front of the door. In that mere millisecond of an opening, I dashed over and snatched her away.

"Run!" I shouted, holding her wrist tightly, and started to run whether she liked it or not. I tossed away my umbrella and headed for the main street at full speed, not caring a bit how this must look.

Hiroka squealed and struggled at first, but at some point, she realized that I was her kidnapper. "Ohh, honestly, Makoto," she said, blithely, and then obediently trotted along behind me.

We left the secluded area of the love hotel and raced down the back alleys until we finally arrived at a bright shopping street. I found a twenty-four-hour doughnut shop and pushed Hiroka inside.

"Can I get a coconut doughnut?" She turned her puppy dog eyes on me.

"Have whatever you want, just order!" I snapped.

Tray in hand, I rushed us up to the second floor, which was practically deserted, maybe due to the late hour. I sat us down at a table in a corner where we wouldn't stand out and finally paused to take a breath.

"Haah." Unconsciously, I stretched out across the top of the table. I was panting, my heart was pounding, and the rain had melted away the hair mousse, leaving my bangs plastered to my forehead.

"Oh, Makoto! You look like one of those *kappa* monsters with their terrible bowl cuts!" Hiroka squealed, carrying on like she was having the best time of her life. Even though she was soaked to the skin just like I was, she looked more like a mermaid lounging on the shore. But this was no time to be dumbstruck by her beauty.

"What the hell? I mean, seriously." Adrenaline still pumping through my veins, I pressed her for answers. "What were you doing with that old man?"

If I'd taken half a second to cool off and actually think about it, I would have known the answer to that question without having to ask it at all. Looking at anything but the reality that was right in front of my nose, I just wanted

Hiroka to say it was all a misunderstanding—I'd happily accept the dad theory or anything else for that matter.

She smiled as she played with her wet hair. "He's my lover," she said, like she was telling me the time of day. She reached out for her coconut doughnut and said, "He sorta came up to me one day an' asked me to be his lover, y'know? So we negotiated a price an' stuff an' here we are!"

"Price?" Completely floored, I leaned into the table and cradled my head in my hands, at my wits' end.

I told you, didn't I? I could almost hear Prapura sighing.

Underneath the dark green jacket, Hiroka wore a tight black knit dress. A gold necklace glittered in the light just above the plunging neckline, and a pair of black lace-up boots finished her outfit off. She was gorgeous, an air of sophistication drifting about her. It was enough to make the 28,000-yen sneakers on my own feet look sad and washed out. But the thought that she'd chosen every bit of it to look good for that old man made me want to rip it all off and throw it out the window.

She was even wearing a bit of makeup. Her eyebrows were neatly shaped, and her sleepy, single-lidded eyes were painted in pearl eye shadow. The tinted pink balm that adorned her lips made them look much fuller, so that they were all the more voluptuous.

The idea that she would use those lips, those eyes, that

immature body to earn money from a man old enough to be her father—it couldn't be true.

While I tried to pull myself together, I merely watched as Hiroka polished off the coconut doughnut.

"Everything I want's expensive, y'know?" She began to talk, sounding more like she wanted to placate me than to make excuses for what she was doing. "Pretty clothes, bags, rings, all those nice things I want are super expensive. Even if I tried to save up my allowance, okay? Even if I saved up for a whole year, I could never buy any of them. I mean, it's all so wildly expensive that I really wonder how they could even cost that much money at all! But if I do it with him three or four times, boom, I can buy whatever I want." She giggled, gleefully.

What on earth could I even say to this cherubic prostitute laughing as she licked bits of coconut powder off her fingers?

"What's wrong, Makoto?" Hiroka smiled innocently, utterly oblivious to how I felt in that moment. "You're all spaced out."

"I really don't get it, you know?" I muttered. "You can't seriously like it, though, right?"

"It?" She raised a neat eyebrow.

"Like, with an old guy like that . . ." *Sex! The sex part!* I hated to even imagine it.

"Mmm." She kept smiling brightly, innocently cheerful.

"I was grossed out by the idea at first, but I guess I'm used to it now. Or maybe it's more like we have this sort of chemistry now. I like doing it now. And he's a pretty nice guy. I really got lucky."

"Lucky?" Now it was my turn to raise an eyebrow.

"It's hit or miss, you know. From what I hear from other girls I think I got really lucky with this guy. He's super generous, and like, even when we're doing it, he—"

"Stop." My voice was unexpectedly rough. "Not interested." *Don't tell me any more.*

To calm myself down a bit, I took a sip of my cold hot chocolate. It was sickly sweet and tasted terrible. Apparently, a lot of things in this world were hit or miss. Makoto's first love was a colossal miss, but even so, I still couldn't bring myself to hate her.

"Hiroka," I said, once I'd more or less pulled myself together. "You really want beautiful clothes and rings and stuff that bad?"

"Yes." She nodded, firmly. "There's nothing else I want."

"You want it all so bad you'd sleep with an old guy like that?"

"I do."

"Can you wait until you're a grown-up?" I was almost pleading with her now. "Until you can earn money properly?"

"I can't! How could I wait?" Her voice grew thorny for

the first time. "I mean, what about you? Could you wait until you're a grown-up for those sneakers? They look expensive."

I gulped and looked down at my feet. The famous brand name glittered and shone on the blue sneakers marked with flashy yellow stripes down the sides.

"For real, Makoto, tell me. You think you're gonna want to wear those when you're like, thirty or forty or something?"

"Uh . . ." Uh-uh, not at all.

"That's how I feel. I want it *all* right now, the beautiful clothes, the bags, the rings. Who cares when I'm a grown-up? I mean, once I'm an old lady, my body'll be worthless. And if my body's worthless, then what's even the point of buying pretty things? When I get so old that only aprons and granny shirts look good on me, then I'll be a good girl and wear the aprons and shirts," Hiroka announced proudly, completely sure of herself, and thrust her chin out defiantly.

To get things that were worth something for the person she was *now* with a body that was worth something now—she had clearly never even considered the idea that there could be anything wrong with this.

"I want to wear beautiful clothes today and I want to feel beautiful every day. Like, this outfit? He gave it to me. It's gorgeous, right? Black's my favorite color. When I'm wearing my favorite clothes, I'm so unbelievably happy that I even feel this sort of unconditional love for the entire human race."

For some reason, I had a hard time looking directly at her dressed all in black and brimming with confidence. It was true that with her fair skin, black looked really good on her. *But, Hiroka. That old man bought you those clothes not so you could dress up in them, but so he could get you out of them.*

"Makoto, are you sad?" Hiroka lowered her voice suddenly.

"Why?"

"It's just like, sometimes, okay? Some people say they get sad when they talk to me."

I totally understood how they felt.

"When people say that, I get sad, too."

"I'm not sad," I lied. "I'm just frustrated."

"Frustrated?"

"If I was rich, I'd buy all your time right now, Hiroka."

Whoa, what am I even saying?! My face started to turn beet red before the words were entirely out of my mouth. I was basically no better than that pervy old man!

But her reply surprised me. "You want to have sex with me?" she asked, the look on her face serious. "We can if you want."

"Huh?!" *We can?!*

"I could do it with you."

"Uh?!" *For real?!* I thought I'd leap up into the ceiling.

And then she struck the killing blow. "Yeah. For you, Makoto, I could do it for just twenty thousand yen."

I couldn't believe my ears. And then I cursed myself for being so naïve, for getting my hopes up so unbelievably easily. My excitement melted away like the mousse from my bangs in the rain. Only my desire for her remained pathetically as strong as ever.

"I do want to sleep with you, Hiroka," I said, feeling a pang of loss as I stared at her adorably full lips, shining peach in the light. "But I won't."

"Why not?"

"I don't want to be like that old man."

After a moment of silence, she shrugged and laughed. "I get it." The smile on her face was unusually awkward. "Okey-dokey. I'm gonna go."

"Go? Go where?"

"Back to him. My phone's been buzzing this whole time." She lifted her cell phone from its place on her lap to show me.

"You're gonna go see him?!" I raised my voice, without meaning to.

"It was pretty fun when you dragged me off like that, Makoto," Hiroka said, as though placating me. "Like I was in a TV show."

"So then don't go," I said.

"But I feel bad for him." She looked down at her phone. "He gave me the money and he was all ready to go."

"That's . . ."

"I have to honor our agreement." She shouldered the expensive brand-name bag and stood up. "Okay, Makoto, see you later."

"Hiroka!"

I have to go after her. I have to chase her down and say something cool to get her to come back. Hurry, go. You have to go.

But it was only the panic that started running in my head. The key part of this whole equation—my feet—didn't move. I just kept fumbling and flailing and Hiroka gradually moved farther and farther away from me. Eventually, she disappeared from view, and as if to take her place, a couple came and sat down at the table next to me. A stern man and a tough woman, both heavyweight class. They polished off their pastries in utter silence, maybe because they were just too hungry to talk. Cinnamon doughnut. Chocolate cream. French cruller. Jelly. Cheese muffin. The coconut doughnut Hiroka liked . . . It was all over now. Too late. I'd completely lost sight of her.

Somewhere, in some cowardly corner of my heart, I was relieved.

6

An unlucky day is unlucky from start to finish, every single minute of every single hour.

My headache only got worse after that, and when I staggered out of the doughnut shop on unsteady feet, the rain was four times as strong as it had been when I went in, sheets of water falling from the sky. And I'd thrown away my umbrella when I'd plundered Hiroka.

I was stuck. I pulled my hood tight around my face and started walking through the bone-chilling nighttime city. The wet asphalt reflected the almost-vulgar colors of the neon signs, as if the ground were soaked in red wine. Herds of people swimming in a wine river, eye-catching couples under a single umbrella, day laborers handing out pocket tissues on pretty much every street corner, touts shouting loud enough to be heard over the rain and the wind and the trains.

I had no strength left in me, and even the drunken laughter rubbed me the wrong way, so my feet naturally turned in a direction where people weren't. I kept walking, moving farther and farther from the crowds, until I passed beyond the warren of meandering alleyways and overhead train lines and came out beside a playground.

It was a lonely little playground, nothing but swings, a slide, and a sandbox. But beggars couldn't be choosers. I could hardly stay on my feet at that point. I sat down on the rusting bench.

Just then I began to shiver violently. The moment I let my guard down and relaxed slightly, the pain attacked my head, I was hit with a ferocious chill, and I felt like throwing up. On the verge of total collapse, I desperately worked to keep myself upright in the incessant rain, while I wondered what I was even doing there in the first place. All I had to do was say yes. I could have been in a warm bed all alone with Hiroka at that very moment. I knew this was actually impossible, but when I thought about it now, I wanted to cry. Because I'd said no, she was alone in a warm bed with a middle-aged man instead . . . When this realization hit me, I really did start to cry.

"I thought you weren't as weak as Makoto Kobayashi?"

The rain above my head stopped abruptly. I looked up to find Prapura's parasol had appeared there at some point, coloring my field of view white.

"Makoto only tailed them. I, on the other hand, went a step farther, so my wounds are that much deeper," I shot back.

"So you regret not sleeping with Hiroka Kuwabara?" I could hear a grin in his voice.

"Of course I do. I totally regret it. I knew I would from the moment I said no."

"But if you'd paid to sleep with her, you would've regretted it more later."

"I know that, too."

"Clever boy." Prapura flashed his teeth in a smile. "You did passably well. At any rate, you won out over temptation."

"Thanks." I showed a few teeth of my own. "But it's actually none of your business. Look, I'll just tell you this now. I'm not especially interested in being clever. I don't particularly care about winning out over anything. And I definitely don't need anyone to come along and tell me how smart I am and act like they've even got a clue what I'm going through."

An evil chill returned to the back of my neck. I wrapped my arms around myself and pulled my body into a ball.

"The problem here is that even though I managed to go and kidnap Hiroka with these very hands, I couldn't take her anywhere. It's not because I'm clever that I didn't sleep with her or go after her. It's because I'm a coward." I squeezed the words out in a hoarse voice.

Prapura rubbed my back. "Cleverness or cowardice, it's your saving grace. First of all, you're only fourteen years old, too early for you to be thinking about trying to rescue anyone. After all, even my boss has a hard time making someone come this way when they're intent on going the other way."

"You can't do it, either? Bring Hiroka home right now?"

"Apologies. I'm an angel, I don't have superpowers."

"Wait." I frowned, slightly. "So then someone with superpowers is better than an angel?"

"I don't know." *Blah blah, grumble grumble.* Prapura trailed off vaguely. "At any rate, my role is to guide, and guide you I will. But I do not carry people. Say if you were lost out here and running a high fever, for instance, I could show you the way home. But you would have to stand up and walk there yourself."

As soon as I heard "high fever," I felt intensely feverish and in even more pain than before. I didn't have the energy left in me to walk all the way to Makoto's house, and even if I had, I couldn't go back there. I could still hear the mother wailing as I walked away. I couldn't go home.

"Can I ask you a question?" I slowly turned my eyes up at the angel. "Can I quit this do-over?"

"You want to quit after a mere month and a half?" He shook his head with a sigh. "Please try to remember. You weren't allowed the first time you asked to 'pass' on your second chance. That rule remains in force. The lottery is absolute."

I groaned. "So then, if I keep going like this forever, totally unmotivated in this life, and I never remember the mistakes I made in my past life, I'll be Makoto Kobayashi forever?"

"There is a limit. Usually about a year."

"*Usually*? What's that about?"

"It's case by case," he replied. "Some people catch on more quickly than others, essentially."

"You'd think you'd have a real rule."

"Well, our industry's managed by the same boss who controls the lower world here."

"I see." This somehow made sense to me. "So what happens to me when the time limit's up?"

Prapura's face tightened. "You fail your do-over and are forever removed from the cycle of rebirth, never to return again. In other words, you won't ever be reborn."

"What happens to my soul then?"

"Your soul slips out of Makoto Kobayashi's body and disappears."

"Disappears."

"Yes. *Fwsh!*"

Fwsh. I envisioned my eensy soul vanishing like the bubbles in a glass of soda. All the hassle, all the problems, all the dead ends—all of it vanishing in an instant, gone forever. *Fwsh!* The image was heartrending and endearing at the same time.

"But then . . ." I gave voice to a question that had been bothering me for a while. "If my soul leaves, what happens to Makoto Kobayashi's body?"

"When your soul disappears, Makoto Kobayashi's physical body will also find eternal sleep," Prapura said, as though it were the most natural thing in the world. "His heart really will stop this time. His body is actually long dead, after all."

I looked at Makoto's body, chilled to the bone, with mixed feelings. It was as pathetic as ever, enough to even make *me* miserable, and I was only borrowing it. Still, though, I felt kind of bad for Makoto when I realized it didn't have long to live either way.

You had nothing good going on, huh?

And now you're gonna die like this . . .

Hiroka. His mother. His father. His malicious brother. His unchanging height. His isolation at school. Even I didn't know which one was the last straw, the thing that pushed Makoto entirely over the edge. Maybe they all tangled up together, growing heavier and heavier with each passing day. And then there were more and more of those heavy days, so that they grew even heavier until finally he couldn't take another step forward.

The rain fell onto my forehead and then slid down my cheeks before dripping down my neck. During this brief moment, I prayed for Makoto for the first time.

When I finished my silent communion, I turned back toward Prapura. "I'm done with the questions. I don't need any more guidance today. I'm not going home. And I'd appreciate it if you could just let me be alone right now." The rain was easing up, so I figured I could just sleep outside tonight.

"You're going to sleep in a place like this on a day like this? Are you in your right mind?" Prapura objected.

But I wasn't having it. "You were the one who just said you can't make someone come this way when they're trying to go the other way." I felt like I wanted to throw it all to the wind, let the cards fall where they would.

He finally gave up the fight. "Listen. You're still not seeing how serious this day is. You're being naïve. An unlucky day is utterly unlucky right up to the very last second. If you're not going to go home, you should at least get out of this playground." The angel then disappeared, leaving me with this ominous prophecy and his parasol.

But I was already drifting off. Plus I thought it wasn't actually possible for the world to hit me with anything worse than what I was already going through. Ignoring Prapura's warning, I lay down on the bench and half passed out into sleep.

An unlucky day is utterly unlucky right up to the very last second.

I came to fully understand what he meant by this when

Colorful

I woke up in the middle of the night to a sharp pain in my head. It felt like the handle of an umbrella slamming into it over and over.

The pain was totally different from the earlier dull throbbing of my headache. The intensity was on an entirely different level. It was like my scalp was being ripped off. The staggering torment was not inside my skull but exploding outward from one side. Where was it coming from . . . ? My eyelids slid open slightly, which was when I learned that I was, in fact, being hit with the handle of an umbrella. I was stunned.

The playground was pitch black, not a single streetlamp around to offer up a pool of meager light. The rain had stopped at some point, and in its place, several pairs of eyes pored over me. Black shadows surrounded the bench, looking down on me. One of them was reaching into the pocket of my hoodie.

Ah! My wallet!

The instant I twisted away in surprise, I was hit with a savage punch to one side.

"Unh!"

It worked. And as a bonus, they stole my wallet.

I curled up, clutching my stomach, and someone's fat hands yanked me up by my collar and began shaking me. And then slapping me. *Whap! Whap!* The sharp hand caught my face coming and going. My cheeks grew hot, and a bolt of electricity shot through my hazy brain.

Dammit, how shitty can this day get . . .

When I came to, I had been dragged down onto the ground. As I tried to crawl away in the muck, the kicks came fast and furious, landing on my back, my arms, my legs. Each time a foot landed on me, I groaned and my cold-numbed fingers twitched. Finally, one of my attackers got on my back like I was a horse, and just as I was about to throw up, someone grabbed hold of my ankles, tight enough to cut off the circulation. There was a yanking on my toes, some tugging, and then my feet were instantly lighter . . . Why?

"Aaaaah!" The second I realized what they'd done, I flipped out. "Give back my sneakers!" I screamed.

I didn't even know why I was freaking out like that. I didn't know I still had that kind of strength left in me. But somehow, I leaped to my feet and challenged the herd of black shadows, fighting back with all the might my small body could muster. "Give my shoes back. Give them back!"

Their only reaction was ridiculing laughter. With a tap to my chest, they flipped me over onto the ground, a move that was quickly followed by a punch to my jaw. When I threw a hand up at the overwhelming shock, my palm came back dyed red with a warm liquid.

Colorful

"I said, give them back!" The familiar taste of blood quickly filled my mouth.

Covered in mud, I kept getting up to throw myself at them over and over, even though they only returned laughter and beatings.

"Give them back! Give my sneakers back! My sneakers! Give them back! Give them back!" As I howled the words, I started to cry, although I knew it was pathetic.

My precious treasure. I'd bought those sneakers with Makoto's savings. I thought they would give me at least a tiny bit of confidence while I was stuck in his body. They were the best life hack I could manage. The world was full of sneakers that cost 100,000 or even 200,000 yen. Why did they have to steal my 28,000-yen kicks?

"You cheap bastards!" I snarled, and the umbrella handle hit the top of my head once more. The world twisted around me, and I fell into the distortion.

"Hey!" Just as I was on the verge of passing out, I heard a voice from far off. "What are you doing?! Stop!" I'd heard this guy's voice before.

"It's the cops!"

Approaching footfalls, fleeing footfalls. The circle of shadows around me disappeared, and in their place, a single shadow shook my shoulders.

"Makoto! You okay?"

Oh, right. That's Mitsuru's voice . . .

"My sneakers . . ." I kept groaning, persistently, unable to let go, even as all the strength drained out of my body now that it seemed that I was finally saved. "My sneakers, okay, the sneakers I, sneakers . . ."

The words played on repeat in my muddled brain, and I felt something push up into my throat abruptly. I didn't have the strength left to stand again, so I vomited with my mouth pressed against the cold sludge on the ground.

Mitsuru stroked my back as he grumbled under his breath.

Once my stomach was empty, the cold abruptly closed in on me, and this time I really did pass out.

7

The constant shudder-sway of the night train. The snow falling beyond the window. The roar of the waves. Hiroka's fair skin.

I immediately knew this was a nightmare.

Hiroka and I were on a night train together. We were apparently eloping and she was laughing, in high spirits— "It's like a TV show." We pressed up against each other fondly, and then our happiness was quickly shattered with all the illogical absurdity of a dream.

The steam train pulled into the terminal station, and the middle-aged man was there waiting for us on the platform. Hiroka's attitude changed instantly.

"I have to go with him."

"Why?"

"Because you're barefoot, Makoto."

With a gasp, I looked down to find that I had no shoes. My 28,000-yen sneakers were gone.

Stunned, I stood rooted to the spot while the

middle-aged man whisked Hiroka away. The chilly station platform. The snow falling on the tracks.

And then the dream flew ahead and away, and before I knew it, the out-of-service night train was rocking me back and forth in my seat as it headed back to the yard.

Even though there were no other passengers, the conductor came through checking tickets. "Your ticket, please."

I held it out, and the conductor shook his head.

"This is the former Makoto Kobayashi's ticket. I need to see the ticket for the current Makoto Kobayashi."

"Are they not the same?"

"They are not. I can tell the difference, even if no one else can."

When I looked, I saw the conductor was Shoko Sano.

Flustered, I got to my feet. I turned my head toward the window and discovered Makoto's mother dancing with the flamenco teacher outside.

What is this place? What the heck happened here?!

I grew increasingly confused. I'd figured out that it was a dream at least, but I couldn't find my way to the real world, no matter how I searched for a doorway. There was no exit that would let me escape from this nasty place.

It was then that I heard someone singing. A man's voice, low and whispered. The song was a sad one, from the north country. Who was it? Who was singing this song in perfect time with the flamenco dancing? Who . . .

Colorful

I opened my eyes and found the face of the father, intoxicated by his own singing voice.

As I woke up to the reality of the Kobayashi house, I realized I was in bed in Makoto's room with the lights off. The father was sitting on the edge of the bed, staring at me. When he met my eyes, he jerked his head back and quickly exited the room, embarrassed to be caught.

The father singing by the bedside of his ailing son?

For an instant, I felt like I was still inside that surreal dream, but then he came back in with medication in one hand. Apparently, this wasn't part of the dream. I wanted to ask him why he'd been singing, but my throat was so sore I couldn't speak.

It wasn't just my throat. As my mind cleared, my whole body started to creak in pain. Plus, I was freezing cold on top of that.

I found out later that the police car Mitsuru had called took me to the emergency room one train station over, where they treated my injuries and did a complete examination on my bleeding head before the parents came to take me home. After that, I'd stayed in a heavy sleep that lasted nearly twenty hours, eventually waking up to the father's song. I still had a high fever, and I felt so nauseated that I basically threw up the cold medicine he gave me as soon as it slid down my throat.

Tortured by the never-ending pain in my head and the

chills that racked my body, I was stuck in bed for the following five days. My fever simply wouldn't go down. By day
two, my stomach still wouldn't accept the cold medicine,
and as a bonus, the cuts all over my body began to fester
and ooze painfully. My beaten face also swelled up like a
swarm of wasps had stopped by for a visit.

Even so, on the third day, I was finally able to keep
the medicine down, and perhaps because of that, my cold
got a little better. I was also able to eat some of the rice
porridge the mother made me, albeit with an angry resistance in my heart. I hated the fact that when push came to
shove, I had no choice but to let this woman take care of
me. I refused to meet her eyes while she replaced the cold
cloth on my forehead with the utmost care, as though she
were atoning for her sins.

It was on this third day that I was first made aware of
how reckless my plan to sleep in the playground had actually been. That area had never been especially safe. There
were constant reports of groups of teenagers stealing wal-
lets and beating people up.

"Even you had to have known that much at least,"
Mitsuru said, yanking me up by my collar when we passed
on the stairs at night. "And since you knew that, I'm guess-
ing you went all the way over there to get beaten up. You
wanna die that bad? Then go ahead and die already. This

house'd be much happier if you were gone. Just don't fuck it up next time."

I didn't think there was any need for him to lecture me, but since he was the one who had saved me, I couldn't really say anything back.

When I didn't come home that night, the mother got worried and asked Mitsuru to help her look for me. He went around all the neighborhoods to see if he could catch sight of me. If he hadn't found me, I might have ended up even worse off.

My fever had dropped a lot by the fourth day, and I was able to eat regular food again, albeit just a little. The swelling in my face was also mostly gone, and disturbingly ugly blue bruises rose up in its place.

As if they'd been waiting for me to recover, two police officers came to take my report the morning of that fourth day. The mother had submitted a damage report the night of the attack. I told them what I could remember of the beating I'd taken, and the police officers wrote every detail down. I barely had any memory of who did it, though, so nothing I said was likely to be very useful in their investigation.

"In junior high with twenty-eight-thousand-yen sneakers, huh?"

"I don't get it, man."

The officers left, scratching their heads in earnest.

I knew that the sneakers were worth that much exactly because adults like them didn't get it. But thinking back, even I couldn't understand why I had been so fixated on those sneakers that night.

I'd recovered more or less by the fifth day, so that standing up and moving around was a whole lot easier. Now moving was a delicious luxury and lying in bed was torture. I was fed up with the life of a sick person by this point. It was on the evening of this day that I had my first visitor.

"Makoto, your friend's come to see you," I heard the mother say from the other side of the door.

And then there was another voice: "Hello!"

The door opened with a clack. When Shoko Sano's face appeared from behind it, my whole being shuddered with horror.

My sworn enemy, 100 percent on the no-way index. On top of that, I was in a pair of shabby pajamas, my hair wasn't moussed up, and I hadn't taken a bath in who knew how long, so I probably stank. Besides, I didn't have the energy to go at it with Shoko. I was at an extreme disadvantage.

"Haven't see you in a while. Are you feeling okay?" She came at me with a grin, but I couldn't bring myself to smile back at her, no big deal.

"Obviously not. That's why I'm stuck in bed." I leaned back against the headboard and welcomed Shoko with my bad mood on full display. "If you're gonna come over, at least call and say you're coming first."

"Ah!" Shoko's eyes grew wide. "Right. The phone."

"We are civilized people, after all."

"Yeah. Sorry."

This meek acceptance wasn't like the Shoko I knew.

She shuffled from foot to foot in the doorway, still wearing her navy duffel coat over her sailor-style school uniform, and with a sigh, I pointed at the desk chair.

"So sit, then."

I regretted it the moment the words were out of my mouth.

"Okay." She set herself down in the chair, looking relieved, and was immediately her usual chattering self again. Meaning she started to talk at me with the intensity of a short-lived cicada. "I heard from Mr. Sawada. He said some guys attacked you in the park? Those bruises are wild! Do they hurt? It looks like they hurt. They have to hurt. That has to be awfully painful!"

"Mm."

"And they stole your wallet, too, right? It was probably some kids from Nishi High. There's been a lot of that lately. Did you report it to the police?"

"Mm."

"You gotta report it. So, like, my dad? He lost his wallet once. It had fifty thousand yen in it, too! But he reported it to the police, and guess what, they actually found it! Three weeks later. Pretty amazing, right?"

"Mm."

"So don't give up. You never know what'll happen. You just gotta report it and keep on hoping—"

"What about the fifty thousand yen?" I interjected.

"Oh. It was gone."

I just stared at her.

She stared back at me.

"Maybe you should leave now?" I urged.

"No way." She squirmed and fidgeted in her seat. "I haven't said what I came to say yet."

"What you came to say?"

She hung her head, at an uncharacteristic loss for words.

Awkward silence. Hot air pumping out of the heater above our heads. Finally, Shoko sat up, and I had a fleeting moment of relief that maybe she was going to leave, after all. But then she rearranged the pleats of her skirt and sat back down.

"A friend of mine says she saw you near the station the night you were attacked."

"Where?"

"The Mrs. Doughnuts on the main street. She said you were with Kuwabara from eighth grade."

My heart pounded faster for a second, but then I realized I didn't actually care. I held my head higher. "So?"

"What?"

"So what if I was?"

"My friend?" Shoko shifted her eyes away from me. "She said Kuwabara's wicked wild, so you better watch out. She said Kuwabara got all these boys at our school to spend a whole bunch of money on her, and then she just dumped them when they had no money left."

"So what if she did?!" I shouted.

"But!" Shoko cried at the same time. "But I do like Kuwabara a lot. I'm not going to stop liking her even if all that stuff is true. That's not what I came here to talk to you about."

I leaned over and pressed my forehead against the duvet. I just couldn't anymore. The more I learned about Hiroka, the less I understood her. I couldn't say for sure that I still liked her.

"So, then," I said to Shoko, almost pleading that she'd give me an answer. "You said you like her? What do you like about her?"

"She comes to art club all the time, right?" she said, her voice quiet. "When she does, the whole room gets so much brighter all of a sudden. Pop!"

"That's it? That's why?"

"I think she has good taste, too. She wanders around the room, and she only ever stops to look at the good paintings. Like how a butterfly flits from one beautiful flower to the next, she only pauses in front of the pretty canvases. And she always stops the longest at yours." Her voice had a honeyish quality to it now, nothing like the way she usually spoke to me. "Kobayashi."

"What?"

"Do you like Kuwabara?" she asked.

"So what if I do?" I replied.

Her mouth tightened the slightest bit. "I've been thinking a lot. Just thinking, you know? And in the end, I thought maybe it's actually not so complicated, maybe it's actually super simple."

"What is?" I raised an eyebrow at her.

"Why you've changed, Kobayashi. They say people change when they fall in love, right? So maybe that's what happened to you. Your love for Kuwabara changed you. If that's what happened, I give up. I decided I would totally give up, even if you never went back to being the old Kobayashi. I came over today to make sure one last time."

The evening sun coming in through the window made her hair shine a deep scarlet.

I was beyond annoyance now. I felt bad for Shoko. She spoke so seriously about this totally wrong idea she had, as if she were possessed by this "old Kobayashi" ghost that only she could see.

I slowly pulled myself back up and sat on the edge of the bed. "Since we're talking about it, I'll ask. How exactly have I changed? What kind of guy was this Makoto Kobayashi you keeping talking about?"

"The Makoto Kobayashi I know always gazed into the depths." Shoko smiled, dreamily. "While all the other boys yell and play like children, Kobayashi's off to one side, quietly focused on the deepest parts of the world. Even in the middle of the noisy classroom or out on the dusty playing field, his eyes alone pick up all those things that no one else notices. You can tell the second you look at his canvases. Don't you remember him? That's the kind of boy Makoto Kobayashi was. A boy who was pure and clear, kilometers away from all the other nasty, childish, rude boys. He took in the sadness of this world and suffered under the weight of it."

Her gaze was fully turned toward the fourth dimension. I could practically see the flowers popping into bloom behind me, almost hear the trilling song of the canaries somewhere.

"Very poetic," I groaned. "But it's a total fantasy." Anger rose up in me, itching at my insides.

"What?" she snapped. "Are you trying to mess with me now?"

"You're the one trying to mess with me. The sort of teenage boy you're talking about doesn't exist."

"Meaning . . . ?"

"Just what I said," I said. "Sorry to break it to you, but

Makoto Kobayashi's always been a regular guy. Not pure, not transparent, just an average teenager. He doesn't live in some fantasy land, either. He lives right here, in the same messed-up world as the rest of you. And yet everyone just jumps to all these conclusions about him, including you. You idolized him, others made him out to be a loser weirdo. It's to the point where the guy can barely make a move at all. That's it. End of story. He's just a regular guy who's a little shy. He worries about the dumbest stuff. He goes and falls in love with the first girl who's a little bit nice to him. He's a regular, stupid guy."

"He's not!" She was angry now, too. "Kobayashi, you're just embarrassed. That's why you're talking like this, trying to make out like it's got nothing to do with you!"

"Okay. Take a look, then!" I pulled incontrovertible evidence out from underneath the bed.

"What're those?" She leaned forward a bit.

"Secret boots. I ordered them," I told her. "I bought them so I could maybe look just a teeny bit taller. I was desperate. That's how pathetic a jerk Makoto Kobayashi is. A totally average fourteen-year-old who obsessively worries about something as stupid as his height. And if that still isn't enough to convince you, then go ahead and open the bottom drawer there."

Shoko gingerly pulled the drawer open and leaped back with a scream. "What is *this*?!"

"It's obvious, isn't it? It's porn. The must-have guide-books for any boy this age. Makoto's got the same desires as anyone else. When night falls, he does what he does. And, you know . . ." A glint in my eyes, I sidled up to her. "He gets certain *ideas* when he's all alone with a girl like this. He also gets pretty horny."

The tanned skin of her throat tensed as she gulped hard. "No way! Kobayashi would never think about that kind of stuff!" she yelled, looking like she would burst out crying at any moment. "You're just being mean on purpose now. You're only saying that stuff to scare me."

"Oh yeah. Wanna try me?" The tears welling up in her eyes. I put a hand on her slender shoulder. "So? How about you try me, then?"

"Stop it, Kobayashi!" she yelled. "Wake up!"

"Oh, I'm awake. My eyes are wide open."

"Your cold'll get worse."

"It'll get better if I give it to you."

Her cherry lips were a size smaller than Hiroka's. I hadn't intended to push this far, but before I could stop myself I started to move in closer to press my own lips to hers.

"Aaaah!" She frantically leaped backward out of the chair.

That scream brought me back to myself.

"What's wrong?" The mother poked her head through the door then, at the worst possible moment, and Shoko fled. She raced out of the room at full speed, and in the blink of an eye, she was nothing more than footfalls disappearing down the stairs.

Suddenly, the room got quiet, and it was just me, the mother, and the tray of tea in her hands. I looked around vacantly until finally my eyes stopped on the mother.

"Cockroach. She flipped out," I said, a poor excuse given that it was very much not cockroach season, and sank down into my bed.

If only the ocean were under this bed, I wished naïvely. If only I could keep sinking down like this, down and down and down forever.

"Idiot." Prapura popped into existence after the mother finally left, and whapped me on the head. "What's the point in ruining a girl's dreams like that?"

And what could I say to that, in the end?

"Can you maybe give me a hint at least?" I asked, dejected. "Was this mistake I committed in my previous life some kind of love affair deal, like rape or a murder of passion or something?"

"Ennnh." Prapura made a large X with his arms and vanished.

My interrogation with regards to the case of Shoko Sano:

Should I have not crushed her dreams?

I don't know.

Should I have pretended to be her rose-colored-glasses version of Makoto Kobayashi?

I can't do that.

But why is she so insistent on wearing those glasses when it comes to Makoto?

Love is blind.

Love? Is Shoko in love with Makoto? Shoko Sano, a girl Makoto hadn't even noticed? No, even if that *were* the case, the Makoto Kobayashi who Shoko was in love with was ultimately an ideal of her own creation. It was an egotistical, fictional love that totally ignored the real Makoto Kobayashi. One way or another, she would have had to learn that such a beautiful and pure fourteen-year-old did not actually exist on this planet.

Broken-down, miserable, kind of a mess maybe, but still we're all doing our best out here.

As I brooded over this in the gloomy room after Shoko's departure, there was someone else under the same roof doing her own fretting and agonizing. And while I quickly got tired of thinking and fell asleep, this other person decided to sit down and put all those thoughts to paper in a letter after some very careful consideration and deep thought. Letter paper was readied and a ball pen sent racing across those pages.

It started like this: "After thinking long and hard, I decided to tell you how I feel in the form of a letter. I know you'd just plug your ears if I tried to sit down and talk to you in person."

And the reason I knew the detailed contents of this letter was because it was addressed to me.

That night, the mother brought supper up a little late and handed me an envelope, looking serious, with the caveat, "Maybe you shouldn't read this. Maybe a mother shouldn't tell her son such things. But I can't fail any harder than I already have. You decide whether or not to read it, Makoto. If you don't want to read it, throw it out, burn it; do what you want with it."

"Can I put it in a bottle and send it out to sea?" I snarked.

"Whatever you want."

I was ready with another sarcastic comment, but it died in my throat when I looked into her eyes. Rather than wavering timidly like it usually did, her gaze was determined, filled with an unwavering resolution.

After she left the room, I tapped the envelope against the tip of my nose. I could smell something extraordinary. The scent of the mother's secret.

Heart pounding, I opened the envelope, and a long letter, spanning eight pages, tumbled out.

8

After those opening lines, it continued:

I really should have told you all of this a lot sooner. But I couldn't work up the courage to do it. I was afraid of traumatizing you, so I just kept putting it off, and here we are now.

I heard you talking with that girl earlier. I could hear your voice through the door when I brought the tea up. You almost never say a word at home, and then there you were, telling this girl exactly what you thought, and rather loudly at that. I just froze in front of the door. I'm sorry for eavesdropping.

It wasn't just the fact that you were talking that surprised me, though. You told her over and over that Makoto Kobayashi was an ordinary boy. You kept saying you were an average fourteen-year-old, although I'm sure the examples of "average" you gave her were a bit too graphic for a girl your age.

She must have been quite shocked by it all,

and so was I. As I stood there listening to you, I started to think that the truth was that I didn't really know a thing about you. Maybe I, too, had been selfishly trying to push you into a mold that I'd created. Maybe I'd unconsciously bound your hands behind your back.

You've always marched to the beat of your own drummer, ever since you were little. It was like you had this neat little world all your own. You didn't have a lot of strength to turn outward to the rest of the world, but for all that, the world you had inside was always rich and full. You were especially good at drawing. Your teachers used to heap praise on you back in kindergarten.

And then your drawings started to win prizes in prefectural and municipal children's art contests, and people in the neighborhood would say such flattering things about you and your talent. I have to admit that it occurred to me then that maybe you were different from the other children, special. Maybe this was a burden to you, but for me, it was a delight.

Instead of "delight," perhaps I should say it made me feel superior. The neighbors would call out to us—"Oh, is this little Makoto, the great artist?" or "He's got a bright future ahead of him, hm?"—and each time a satisfied smile would spread across my face, even if I knew they were just saying it to flatter me. In my heart, I would tell them, "That's right. My youngest boy is different from *your* children."

Because you were the only thing in my life that was special.

Maybe you don't care about any of this. But please listen. I'm not like you. I've always been so average, a girl with no special talents or strengths. I was born to an office worker and a housewife, I had an easy life in a peaceful home, and I finished school without ever going through a rebellious phase. And then I didn't think too much about anything, really. I got older, found a job somehow, and before I knew it, I was the married mother of two.

Such an incredibly average life. But maybe that's exactly why, somewhere deep in my heart, I've always wanted something out of the ordinary. I was always so jealous of people at school or at work who were special in some way—people who excelled at sports or who gained some unique skill. I used to wish I had something like that. No, I tried to believe I did have something like that in me.

Having a child with an artistic talent gave me

just the tiniest bit of confidence. I started to think that since you, my son, were special, I as your mother undoubtedly had something in me, too.

Do you remember when I took those ink-painting classes in the neighborhood just a little before you started first grade? It was right around that time that I began to seriously seek out this vague, hazy something. I wasn't just a housewife, I wasn't just a mother. I wanted to find someone else in me, a totally different self I hadn't even met yet.

Unfortunately, I don't have the same passion for art that you do, and I didn't last long at the ink-painting classes. But once I took that first step, I picked up steam and tried so many classes: an incense-blending course, hula dance, easy epic poetry, sommelier lessons, an introduction to coffee fortune-telling, a caricature class, beginner's Buddhist sculpture, an ESP development seminar, foot pressure points, Mrs. Tanaka's Cooking Fun, starter pantomime, Enjoy Arabic with *Arabian Nights*, weaving flower baskets from vines, Edo-style *kappore* dancing . . .

I wonder if you understand. While this is a history of the challenges I've taken on, it's also a catalogue of my disappointments. I was clumsy and awkward at everything I tried. I always felt like I was so much worse than everyone else in the class, and that would be the end of it. I'd start looking for a new class to take. I repeated this cycle over and over again.

Your dad said he was just happy to see me so full of life after I started taking all the classes. But personally, I was desperate. I struggled with the fear and anxiety that I would grow old with nothing to show for it, so I kept searching. I clung to the idea that this time for sure, this time for sure, I would find the thing that was right for me. But the years simply passed cruelly with all my efforts ending in vain.

Last year, Mrs. Aizawa, a friend from the hula dance class, asked me if I wouldn't go with her to flamenco lessons. For seven years, I'd been searching, pushing myself, fighting so hard for that mysterious something. And after all of that, I decided to give up the search. It was too late. I was tired. I would live and die as an ordinary housewife.

At the time, I had such trouble accepting this that it even kept me awake at night. I had terrible insomnia. But now that I had reached that point, now that I was thinking like that, I was able to simply enjoy flamenco class, without that extra pressure.

It was so fun. I'd never enjoyed learning any-thing that much before. When I moved my body to the lighthearted beat, I felt like I'd been sud-denly freed from those seven years of struggle. Just when I'd lost hope in my own self, flamenco gave me strength. It inspired me and gave me the energy to live. Flamenco taught me that the blinding sun was still shining outside, even when I was sinking into darkness inside the house.

With your sharp intuition, I suppose you've already picked up on this, but there was also the matter of our instructor.

I don't want to make excuses here. My path to flamenco class and my relationship with our teacher are two totally separate things. As a mother, it wouldn't be right for me to talk to you about the latter, but rest assured, I will never forget the fact that I hurt you. I intend to carry that burden for the rest of my days. Whatever my reasons, I should never have done such a thing. And above all else, I should never have made you suffer because of it. I know I can't apologize this away, but let me say that I really am very sorry.

The fact that I was so completely taken up with myself during these seven years fills my heart with just as much regret. This was one of the most important periods for you as you grew bigger each day, and I failed to see the concerns and problems you had as an average boy. Looking back at my pilgrimage of lessons like this now, I'm made painfully aware of the fact that there were so many other things closer to my heart that I should have been paying attention to.

At the same time, I wanted you to get at least a glimpse of how sad it can be to be born with no special talents. I wanted you to see how marvelous it is to have been born with a unique something. Perhaps I simply see you with a mother's doting eyes, but I wish you could take a little more pride in your own uniqueness. I'm not just talking about art, either. I mean that rich inner world of yours and how keenly sensitive you are, too.

After all, I've been proud of you for all fourteen of these years.

After your suicide attempt, I immediately broke it off with my instructor and stopped going to flamenco. All I want now is to find the path where I can live together with you as a mother, as a housewife. Maybe you'll turn your back to me. Maybe you'll say, "It's too late now, leave me alone." Maybe you'll ball this letter up and throw it in the trash. But I write this letter prepared for all those possibilities, with the hope that you'll someday share your anger, your contempt, your hatred, your everything with me, too, the way you opened yourself up to that girl.

I will wait for you forever.

I love the parts of you that are average and the parts of you that are not with all of my heart.

Mom

It was a really long letter.

But for all its length, the crucial bit about the flamenco teacher was still ambiguous. You couldn't exactly call this an absolutely honest confession. I also thought she was just pushing her own selfish excuses on me. She wrote eight pages of this stuff, but was she actually sorry for anything? It didn't really feel like it to me.

Hey, Makoto. Are you satisfied with this? I asked my stomach, head hanging, but Makoto's body didn't respond. It was too late. It was even later than the mother thought, much too late to put anything back the way it was.

I bit Makoto's lip. The thin skin ruptured and I tasted his blood. Makoto's hand didn't want to put the mother's letter in the garbage can, so I left it inside a desk drawer. But that didn't put an end to my irritation.

"So is this what you're trying to say, then?" I promptly

started running my mouth off, the second I saw her face when she came to clear away the supper dishes two hours later. I knew the words that jumped out of my mouth without any real thought weren't going to be pretty. "Basically, you wanted something special, so you went looking for it. And you searched and searched and searched and landed on the most ordinary special thing ever, a married woman having an affair?"

The mother closed her eyes briefly and thought a moment. "I'm done with that role," she said, finally. "Now I'm taking a hard look at the role of mother one more time."

"Mother. The most ordinary of ordinary."

"Extraordinary joy and sadness can come out of the ordinary every day. You let me experience both of these. I was so happy, so, so happy when you started breathing again in the hospital after you died for those ten minutes. I'll never be able to thank those doctors and nurses enough. And I'm grateful to your father, too, from the bottom of my heart for holding me up like that when I was on the verge of madness with grief and fear." Tears sprang up in her eyes.

"Huh." I poured cold water on her little moment. "That selfish man?"

"Selfish?" She frowned.

"Don't play innocent with me. You went looking for an affair because you finally got fed up with his enormous ego, right? He's a hypocrite, only good on the outside; inside, he's devious, unscrupulous. You were sick of him and all of this, so you went chasing after his polar opposite, that Latin guy."

"Now, hold on a minute here. What do you mean?" The mother appeared to have absolutely zero clue what I was talking about. Her face grew serious as she argued back. "Your father is not selfish or hypocritical. He's a good person. He's so good, in fact, I get frustrated with him sometimes."

"Whatever." I wasn't interested in a serious discussion. "I guess that's it for your honest confession, huh?" I jerked my chin in the direction of the door. "Can you just go already?"

"Wait, Makoto. You've got it all wrong. Let me talk to you."

"My head hurts."

"But—"

"My fever goes up when I talk to you," I snapped, but the mother stayed rooted to the spot, like a ghost with unfinished business. When I turned my back on her and dived under my duvet, she finally stepped out of the room and walked away. The final act of a long, long day.

This world was exhausting.

9

I started going to school again the following Monday. Although I was completely over my cold, my face was still covered in bruises, and on top of that, I had to go back in Makoto's ugly old sneakers after my new ones were stolen from me. The utter dejection that filled my heart was a lot like how I felt when Prapura led me to school two months earlier.

But to my surprise, my classmates reacted a bit differently this time. Whereas no one so much as tried to approach me when I first came back to school, now several people spoke to me—"It's been a while," "You okay now?" Stuff like that. There were still a few who gaped at me like I was a pregnant alien, but a quick glance around the classroom showed me that they were in the minority now. The biggest reason for this was the fact that everyone had gotten tired of me and lost interest.

"It's just, like, you're easier to talk to now." Saotome told me the second-biggest reason. "Before, you were, I dunno. It was like you had this total attitude. You seem more chill."

This carefreeness stemmed from the fact that I wasn't the real Makoto Kobayashi, but rather a Makoto Kobayashi with an expiration date, but of course, I couldn't tell Saotome that.

Saotome was the guy who'd asked me how much my sneakers had cost back when I first got them. Of all the people in Grade Nine Class A, he was the one most likely to strike up a conversation with me (except for Shoko, obviously). He wore his longish, slightly curly hair slicked back, which definitely didn't do him any favors. But I'd kind of had hopes for him for a while now, just from the warm sound of his name.

And now he came all the way over to my desk to talk to me on this first Monday back. "I heard they got your sneakers?"

"Yeah." I nodded. "Totally sucks. I really liked them."

"Well, o'course you did. That blows. They were so expensive. I seriously hate guys who gang up on people like that."

"Right? Me, too."

"Like, don't hide behind your buddies. Come at me on your own, y'know?"

"Totally. Although I'm pretty sure even if it had been just one of them, they woulda still kicked my ass."

We both fell silent for a moment.

"You know that shoe place Gomen Soro by the station?" Saotome's eyes lit up as he asked me this question out of the blue, like he was telling me the location of a secret treasure.

"Gomen Soro?" I shook my head. "Never heard of it."

"No one ever has, but it's amazing. Shoes that are normally eight thousand yen or so, they sell 'em for like two thousand."

"Whoa." That *was* cheap. At those prices, I might be able to buy a new pair, even after depleting Makoto's savings like I had.

"You want to check it out?" he asked.

"Yeah," I answered.

And so the next day after school, we got on the bus and headed for the shoe store. It was in a narrow alley off the main street, small but with a huge selection, crammed with high school and university students on their way home.

"When you first walk in you gotta say 'gomen soro,'" Saotome told me, so I did and everyone in the store laughed at me.

The prices were definitely way cheaper than at other stores. After a lengthy period of fierce indecision, I finally bought a pair of white sneakers with green stripes for 2,180 yen. The retail price was 5,600 yen. They were a serious step down from my 28,000-yen sneakers, but Saotome told me they still looked top of the line if you stepped back five meters. More important than anything else, the soles were about a centimeter thicker than on any of the other shoes.

"That's how you decide? It's just a centimeter." The beanpole of a sales clerk laughed, but Saotome didn't. That centimeter was precious to me.

On the way home, I treated Saotome to some fried chicken at the convenience store by way of thanks, so then he treated me to a steamed bun to thank me for my thanks, and I went home satisfied with a full stomach. After that day, the two of us were basically thick as thieves.

"Saotome? You should get some mousse in that hair of yours and part it to one side," I would advise.

He'd counter with his own bit of help for me. "Speaking of mousse, I wanted to say something before, aren't you using too much on those bangs of yours?"

We got this kind of comfortable connection going. We could worry about our hair all we wanted, but in terms of the overall class structure, we were both firmly in the not-hot group. Even so, I wasn't miserable anymore.

Miserable was having to spend lunch hour by yourself, walk to your next class alone. The sheer fact that there was someone next to me every time I turned to look made me just plain happy. My heart practically exploded.

It made me even happier to learn that Saotome's grades were as bad as mine. Just like Makoto found meaning in the art club, Saotome had devoted every day up until summer holidays to the table tennis team. He hadn't ever gone to cram school, either. Plus, his parents were also insisting he go to public school. They said it was a waste of money to send him to private school. They probably had more money than Makoto's parents if they were making the argument that it was a "waste" rather than any particular lack, but on the point where he was expected to make it into a public school, we were facing the same pressure.

Putting it all together, we naturally ended up studying for the exams with each other. We'd stay in the library alone after school, or I'd go over to his house to study. At last, I was truly living like a real ninth grader facing the terrible trial of high school entrance exams.

With just over three months to go before the public school test, I thought it was maybe too late to start scrabbling for a pass. It was probably too late. But for me—or rather for Makoto Kobayashi—it was completely and fundamentally too late in every way. If I started listing all the things I was too late for, I'd never finish.

Thinking about it, this didn't just apply to Makoto. Maybe the world was actually filled to the brim with things it was simply too late for, things we couldn't take back.

The sneakers I'd never get back.

The mother's affair.

Hiroka's body.

Shoko's dream.

And my previous life . . .

"If we'd been born five thousand years earlier,"

Saotome said, while we were studying history one day, "we'd, like, build tools out of stone, and everyone'd build houses together. We'd be eating the hearts of animals we hunted ourselves while they were still hot, y'know? I wish I could've gotten my start in a time like that."

I totally understood how he felt.

While my days at school grew brighter, life with my host family continued in darkness. My relationship with the mother didn't change a whit after that letter of hers, and the father worked constant overtime just as he had before. In addition to that, annoyingly, Mitsuru had apparently decided that it was more fun to come hassle me than ignore me.

"I hear you finally started studying?" He poked his head into my room to spew his venom again one evening about two weeks after I got over my cold.

"Don't just come in." I turned around for a second, thinking it was Prapura, and quickly turned my back again when I saw Mitsuru's grinning face.

"Oh-ho! You're really studying?" He didn't so much as bat an eyelid at my protest. "Whoa. This is a rare sight. It's like, I dunno, you never see this kinda thing in the wild. Mind if I take a pic?"

"Do whatever you want."

"As if. Idiot. Like I'd want a picture of you. Anyway, I

heard your synthesized score is horrible. Sort of pointless putting up a fight at this stage of the game, though?" He just kept coming at me.

"It's, like, ninety percent pointless," I declared, confidently. "But that's not the point."

"Then what *is* the point?" he sneered.

"None of your business."

"Tight-lipped as ever. Not to mention, you've always been so frickin' stubborn. You're like a wild boar—once you start running, you got no brakes. I hear you've got the lights on every night until like three or four in the morning?"

That was true, but I didn't answer him. I was thinking about something else totally.

I haven't actually seen Prapura lately . . .

"Well, *I* don't care, but Ma's worried about your raging-boar style. I think she thinks you lost your mind after they asked you to try for a public school, like you're backed into a corner and the pressure's too much for you. You're such an idiot. You just jump in with both feet, even though you're totally not used to studying like this. You don't have any balance, you're always taking things to the extreme. Rein it in already. Those bags under your eyes get any darker, you'll make the air in this house even harder to breathe. Just stop it."

I ignored him and continued to flip through my vocabulary cards.

"And," he added, "would it kill you to be nice to Ma for five seconds? She's totally on edge lately. This isn't easy for her, either, you know."

"I can't be nice to her."

"What?"

"But I won't make trouble for her, either," I said. "If I don't get into public school, I won't go to a private school. I'll take a gap year."

"Are you seriously that stupid?" he groaned. "Who even takes a gap year before high school in this day and age?"

I was indeed that stupid. But I was also dead serious. "It's fine. I'm a spirit out of sync with this day and age, anyway."

"Huh?"

"I've never been right for this modern Heisei era."

"Uh-huh." He rolled his eyes. "So then what era *are* you right for?"

"The Jomon era, the hunter-gatherer days."

Mitsuru burst out laughing. "That far back? Idiot. Would a Jomon-era spirit cry when someone stole its twenty-eight-thousand-yen sneakers?"

"Sh-shut up!" I snapped. "A Jomon person'd cry if someone stole their terra-cotta statues. It's the same thing. Those sneakers were my terra-cotta statues. They were priceless."

"Those terra-cotta statues are from way after that,

from the Yamato era, you dolt," he informed me, haughtily. "They didn't exist in the Jomon. You really would be better off if you just died and got reborn, huh?"

"You go first." I threw my vocab book at him and he dodged it deftly, laughing loudly as he left my room. And in a bit of perfect meddling, he told the parents about my intention to take a gap year.

First thing the next morning, the mother was crying all over me. "Please, Makoto. Forget about what we said before. We'll work the money out somehow. Please don't worry about it. You just focus on getting into whatever private school you think you can."

But I wasn't about to say yes to this. For one, I didn't love it when people unilaterally changed what they wanted from me. And besides, I had my own ideas.

Basically, this was where I was coming from. Prapura said my homestay had a time limit of one year. At this point in time, nearly three of those months had passed already. High school was another four months off. Which meant that no matter what high school I went to, it worked out that I would be attending it for a mere five months. Public school was one thing, but it was ridiculous to move on to a private school and pay that kind of exorbitant tuition for that period of time.

My reasons were perfectly sensible, but unfortunately, these reasons couldn't be an explanation to anyone other than me. Not a single person in my life was going to take me seriously when I told them I only had another nine months to live. In which case, my only option was to keep my mouth shut and study as hard as I could, so that I somehow managed to get into public school.

And that's exactly what I did. Kept my mouth shut and studied my brains out.

Studying was just boring. It wasn't hard at all, not compared with a marathon or a soccer match or something. The ongoing lack of sleep might have been hard on my body, but it was nothing when I thought about the pain of the night when I was attacked in the park.

The only really hard part of the whole thing was that I didn't have the time to paint anymore, although I couldn't say it was entirely because of the studying that I stopped showing up for art club. I was also avoiding Hiroka and Shoko.

I hadn't been able to stop thinking about the whole thing with Hiroka, and it definitely wasn't that I didn't want to see her. But I had no idea what I would even say to her after all that. My heart sank when I thought about how she could twist me around her little finger without even trying. And it didn't upset or excite me the way it used to when I spotted her at school lately. If things could just sort of fizzle out like this, I was basically fine with that.

Shoko, on the other hand, was in the same class as me,

so I saw her every day. But things had been awkward and uncomfortable between us ever since she came to visit me. She'd chased after me so persistently before, but now she kept her distance (naturally). If our eyes did happen to meet, she would quickly look away. It seemed like it really was her fictional Makoto Kobayashi that she liked, as seen through her rose-colored glasses. I did feel kind of bad for crushing her beautiful ideal, though, and I tried to stay out of her way as much as I possibly could.

And so I pulled back from the world of oil painting and warped into the land of entrance exams with that blue painting still only half finished.

This life was more painfully dull than I had even realized, apparently. Bombarded by kanji characters and an endless parade of numbers, my colorless days were starting to make me feel empty and monochrome.

So maybe it was because my life was so painfully bland that I couldn't reject this sudden invitation when the father came to me, one morning in early December. "This Sunday, it looks like I'll be able to take it easy for the first time in a while. I was thinking of going fishing. How about it? Why don't you come along, Makoto? If you're not interested in fishing, you can just sit next to me and sketch or something."

I twitched in reaction to the word *sketch*.

"I know this little place where the water's nice and

clear. The air's fresh, the view's wonderful. I'm sure you could draw something nice."

The father deftly appealed to my desires. I'd been wanting to draw some landscapes for a while now.

Even so, I held my ground out of stubbornness. "But I have the exams."

"Come on, now." He smiled. "You need a change of pace every so often, right? It's a known fact that you do better after a break, and that goes for both studying and work. So? How about it? Why not just give it a go? It's not that far in the car, and it'd be nice to take a drive. Plus, a nice clear stream in winter, all crisp and sharp, just lovely. All right! We'll head out Sunday morning."

The plan was somehow settled before I knew it, before I had even given any kind of real answer.

I kind of got the feeling he'd backed me into a perfectly laid trap. I headed out of the house for school, feeling unsatisfied with how the whole thing went down, a little grumpy somehow.

On my way home, I scraped together what little remained of my allowance and bought a sketchbook.

10

Early Sunday morning, December 6, 6:30 a.m.

The curtains had just started to shine with the light of daybreak, and when I opened the window, the sky looked like a perfect blue canvas. A foundational layer of blue with nothing painted on it yet. The few faint clouds I could see drifting above the apartment block off in the distance made it look like someone had taken an extremely fine brush to the scene.

What a beautiful day. I exhaled a white breath, mixed emotions welling up in me. The moment I pulled the curtains back, the possibility of the outing being canceled due to rain vanished. It touched a nerve when I thought about the inevitable look of glee on the father's face, but on the flip side, there was a part of me excited enough about the trip that I'd woken up early.

I still had plenty of time before the 7:30 departure. It took me no time at all to get ready. I went back to my room, closed the curtains, opened them, opened my new sketchbook, closed it. I couldn't settle down. Finally, I sat on the edge of the bed and looked up at the ceiling.

"Prapura?" I said, quietly, but there was no answer. "I got something I want to talk to you about."

No answer.

"How are my bangs today?"

I kept speaking to him and he kept not showing up. Now that I was thinking about it, I realized it had been more than three weeks already since I'd seen his face.

Hey, Prapura. Where'd you run off to? You skipping out on your job? Or does this mean your role as my guide's finished now?

I'd kind of had this vague sense that things were changing lately, what with Saotome guiding me to the shoe store and the father guiding me off somewhere today. Which is, in fact, why I was scared.

Where exactly were these earth people taking me?

With the father behind the wheel, the navy Toyota Caldina pulled away from the city on the two-lane street, and then out onto the four-lane national highway until it merged onto the six-lane expressway to leave the prefecture itself, eventually carrying us onto a twisting mountain road.

The whole "it's not that far by car" was a complete lie; the entire trip easily took three hours. I never once opened my mouth. Instead, I leaned up against the window of the passenger seat and pretended to sleep, but before too long, I really did fall asleep.

When I opened my eyes, the car was driving through a small town in the valley. Fields spread out in the space between mountains, houses dotted the land between them, and the road was unobtrusive, as if trying not to disturb this tranquil scene. The village was so quiet. From time to time, I'd catch sight of signs for *onsen* hot springs or karaoke parlors, but for some reason, I never found the actual buildings for these places. Eventually, the signs disappeared, too, and just when the world around us was becoming increasingly desolate, the father stopped the car on the deep shoulder of a gravel road.

"Well, around here's good enough, I guess," he said, pinching the bridge of his nose. But the gravel road was surrounded by thick stands of trees, and I couldn't see the merest hint of a river.

Welp, I thought as I opened the passenger door. An unspeakable chill slammed into me, numbing my whole body, like someone'd just sprayed me with ice water.

"You have to wear some proper warm clothes," the father said, sagely, now of all times, as he pulled his fishing gear out of the trunk. Perhaps he also realized how too-little, too-late this piece of advice was; he pulled his scarf off and pushed it toward me.

I refused it. A hand-knitted scarf was just too tacky,

and it wasn't like it was so cold I couldn't stand it. It was indeed chilly out here, but the verdant air was so clear, it more than made up for the low temperature.

"Okay, then. Let's get going." The father gave up on trying to get me to take the scarf and wound it back around his neck before stepping into the trees.

I followed with my sketch tools in one hand. We walked down a gentle slope, brushing away the branches that blocked the path forward. There were still droplets of morning dew on the leaves, and when I looked up, the sunlight filtering through the branches dazzled my eyes.

After about ten minutes, the view opened up to reveal the river that was apparently our destination, a small, clear stream flowing soundlessly across a desolate field. Bathed in the morning light, the surface had a green patina to it, and I felt a pang of disappointment at the possibility that the water was stagnant. But taking a closer look, I saw that the coloring came from the plants swaying back and forth just beneath the river's surface. The water itself was so crystal clear, I could see all the way down to the sand of the riverbed. A majestic forest sprawled outward from the shore on both banks, while the shadow of a snowcapped mountain rose up above the stream.

I had to admit that the view was really something. It wasn't the sort of scene that would make a perfect picture from every side, but I could probably turn it into a picture with the right angle and composition. It was maybe even the ideal spot for sketching. But . . .

"Can you actually catch anything here?" I turned cold eyes on the father, who was already clutching his fishing rod at the river's edge. I couldn't see any sign of fish, and anyway, there were too many plants in the water for fishing.

"Whether or not I catch anything is secondary," he announced. "I'm here to lie around by the river and enjoy the view. That's how your dad fishes. The fish don't matter at all. Ha ha!"

The father seemed serious about ignoring the fish. He'd come all this way to catch something in the river, but he hadn't brought a bucket or a cooler. He settled himself down heavily by the edge of the river, lowered his rod into the water—no bait on the hook—and just spaced out. Every so often, he'd grin to himself, although I had no idea what was so funny.

What a strange man. Paying him no mind, I looked for a place to sketch and then laid out my picnic tarp in a sunny spot with a good view. I sat down and quickly opened my brand-new sketchbook. Within five minutes of setting my pencil to work, a chill came creeping in from all sides, starting at the tips of my fingers and crawling up my arms, from my toes to my thighs, my butt to my stomach. Drawing outdoors in the middle of winter was harsh. Even so,

I enjoyed the sketching itself, and before I knew it, I was utterly absorbed in the work.

The clarity of the river.

The majesty of the trees.

The breeze playing on my skin.

I still didn't have the ability to really bring these to life in my drawings, but from time to time, when I drew the leaves on the tree, I could almost touch them on the page, and when I sketched the quiet current, I felt my fingertips sink into that cool water.

It was like the leaves of the trees pushed a heavy weight away, like the water of the river cleansed my insides and something started flowing again. I finished the rough sketch, and as I added pigment and hue with my watercolors, I could feel my body steadily growing lighter, the extra weight pressing down on my shoulders lifting. Maybe I was even more tired than I'd thought from all the studying.

My brush moved along at a good pace, and every few minutes, the father came over to peer at the painting as it unfolded in my sketchbook. He'd push his scarf on me again every time before he turned and headed back to his own spot.

At the end of the morning, I'd finished one painting, and he hadn't caught a single fish.

"You only do landscapes then, Makoto?" he asked me

at lunch, as we spread out on my picnic tarp the food the mother had packed for us. "You don't do portraits?"

"No." I shook my head and warmed myself up with coffee from the thermos.

"Why not?"

"I hate people," I replied, curtly, and instantly I saw Saotome's face in the back of my mind, so I added, in a small voice, "Generally."

"Hm. You do?" Nodding and humming his agreement, he picked up a rice ball and polished it off in four bites. He then tossed some fried egg, a wiener, and a mini hamburger into his mouth one after the other before finally turning back to me.

"I generally hate people, too." The smile on his face was cheerily blithe. "For a while, I really hated them, you know."

"Oh yeah?" I said, without much enthusiasm, and threw some fried chicken into my mouth. The flavor of soy sauce spread out across my tongue, and as I enjoyed the lingering aroma, I reached out for a rice ball.

"Do you know why I asked you to come fishing today?" the father asked, as he crunched on some pickled daikon.

"I do."

"Huh. You do, then?"

"I said I do. You pretended we were going fishing so you could get some time to talk to me."

He stopped his daikon-crunching. "So you're onto me."

"Saw right through you."

Father-son fishing trip equals talk time. I figured he had this kind of sitcom-style ulterior motive in planning this whole outing.

"Well, that makes this all that much easier, then." He looked somewhat relieved. "You're exactly right. We came out because I wanted to talk to you, Makoto. I've been holding off on sitting you down in the hope that you might come to me yourself, but I've been thinking lately, what if I wasn't waiting for you so much as running away from you? Not to mention, it's hard on me to see your mom in such low spirits these days."

I just stared at him.

"I don't know what happened between the two of you," he continued. "But you do start to wonder when you're all under the same roof together and things between your wife and son go all pear-shaped."

"As a son, you do start to wonder when your parents act like everything's just fine and dandy, but they're really only going through the motions of being husband and wife," I snarked, suddenly feeling spiteful.

"What's that supposed to mean?" He raised an eyebrow at me.

"Nothing."

"No, tell me," he insisted. "Go ahead and lay it all on me."

"Okay, I'll just say it, then," I started. "Wasn't it a huge mistake for you to marry her?"

"Mistake?"

"I was just thinking maybe you regret it."

"That's just ridiculous." He frowned, immediately serious. "I've never once regretted marrying your mother. Just the opposite, in fact. I feel like I'm blessed. I'd never be able to find another partner like her."

I wanted to tell him that was because he didn't know who she really was, but he kept going in a loud voice.

"She's just so full of life, you know? Unlike your old homebody dad. I'm not interested in much of anything, but your mom, she's always up for a new challenge. I'm sure you remember, too, Makoto. She keeps on trying one new thing after another, from epic poetry to *kappore* dancing. I really admire her enthusiasm, how positive she is. You have no idea how much strength her vitality gives me."

"Huh." My mouth hung open, and I looked up into space.

Up for a challenge. Positive. Vitality.

I hadn't seen even a whisper of any of these ideas in that overwhelmingly despairing letter from the mother. But the father apparently seriously believed this was what she was like.

"I'm not just talking about her hobbies. Uh-uh. With

that part-time job of hers, too, she's a fountain of energy. She never stops smiling. It's like she has just as much fun there as she does with her classes. She really kept me going when I was out of work. I don't know what I would've done without her."

Part-time job? Out of work?

More new past came flying at me.

Whoa, whoa. What exactly are we talking about here?

"And I'm not just talking financially. Mentally, too. I was completely worn out back then. I couldn't have made it through all that without your mom's cheery smile."

I was utterly baffled, as the conversation pushed ahead in an even more unexpected direction, leaving me behind.

"Now, I never really talked to you or Mitsuru about all this back then, back when I was really at my lowest. I didn't want to sit around complaining, and I didn't want to worry you guys either, so I never said anything. But maybe, at the end of the day, I was actually trying to keep up appearances. After you tried to commit suicide, I really regretted not telling you the whole story. I shouldn't have put up a strong front like that, I should have made more of an effort to talk to you, not just about this, but about all my worries, my weaknesses. Even if it wasn't particularly helpful to you then, I should have at least talked to you. Maybe you'll hear me out now?"

I realized suddenly he had the wheel in this conversation

and was driving me in the direction he wanted to go. I was dumbfounded, but before I had the chance to protest, he set about talking in earnest.

"I had to quit my old job at the candy company back when you were still in elementary school. That was the start of my misfortune. I told you boys that I quit to take responsibility for a mistake at work, but the truth is, that was only half the story. There *was* a mistake, but it was my boss's and I took the fall. Happens all the time."

A self-deprecating smile spread across his face. This wasn't like him.

"Because my boss bungled things, we were back to square one for a contract with a major chain store. Next thing I knew, the blame for the whole mess had been put squarely on me. Plus we'd been in the red for a while, and the company was looking for people to downsize. But it wasn't getting fired that hit me the hardest. I'd trusted that boss and he betrayed me."

"Is that why you started hating people?" I asked, hesitantly.

"Maybe it wasn't so much that I hated them as I got scared of them. Everyone in the office knew the truth of the situation, and yet not one of them so much as opened their mouth to speak up for me."

As he spoke, the cypress leaves fluttered in the breeze above his head, and every so often, a bird chirped. The noon sun even farther up rained its dazzling golden particles down on us.

"On top of that, the country was in the middle of a recession, and I couldn't seem to line up my next job. Even so, if possible, I wanted to keep doing the project-development work I'd been doing at my old job. I really love the process of thinking up new products and bringing them to life. It's only thanks to your mother that I could indulge in that kind of thinking. It's because she was right there by my side, cheering me on, that I could take my time and look for the right job. I was unemployed for around six months, until I was finally able to restart my career in the project-development division of the company where I work now. And I was over the moon when I got the job. I figured your mom could finally go back to those lessons she loves."

His voice bounced up for an instant, but fell sharply. "However, your dad's misfortune wasn't quite over. Because then my new company got caught up in some pretty serious trouble."

Trouble—the fraud I'd heard so much about.

"You seriously have zero luck, Dad."

I'd been listening absentmindedly to him as he painted himself as the victim, and now I gasped in sudden horror. I couldn't let myself be taken in. After all, this "trouble" ended with him getting promoted from a rank-and-file office worker to the division manager. He had to have been literally dancing for joy that night when the company CEO and the board of executives were all rounded up.

"You worked there. Did you really not know about the fraud stuff?" I looked at him warily. "Weren't you actually involved in the whole scam?"

The look on his face was hard to read. "I didn't know when I first started working there. Or I should say, the CEO was still on the straight and narrow back then. He's a bit of an oddball. He's always saying sales isn't about selling a product, it's about selling an idea. And he was ambitious even then, but he wasn't doing anything that came close to breaking the law. Then, about two years ago, things started to look bad when he began pursuing this extreme theory that you can get consumers to come on board so long as the idea is good, even if the product itself is junk. Word started going around the office that he'd launched a pretty iffy project with some trusted directors. I guess they figured they could keep it top secret, but people in the office were bound to figure it out, no matter how well they actually hid it."

"So then you *did* know."

"Mm-hmm." He nodded. "There wasn't anyone at the company who didn't."

"If you knew, then why didn't you stop it?"

"I tried to any number of times. I appealed directly to

the CEO and his cronies whenever they launched some dodgy scheme. I said that if we kept doing things like this, we were going to be facing some serious consequences down the road. I said we should be putting our efforts into developing actual products, even if it took more time."

"Huh." Something was off here. This wasn't the story I knew. Prapura hadn't said a word about any of this.

"The CEO turned on me. It was just like what happened at the candy company. My desk was moved, off by a window in an out-of-the-way corner of the office, and they stopped giving me any work to do. They were trying to shame me, to force me up against the wall, make it so I had no other option but to submit my resignation. I didn't, though, maybe out of sheer spite. But if I lost this job, I didn't know when I'd find another one again. And of course, I couldn't do that to your mother. We still had the mortgage on the house and the tuition fees for you boys. They could strip my pride if they wanted to. I'd still get paid my salary so long as I kept going into the office."

He let out a heavy sigh. "Two years," he said. "I went to work every day like a dead man for two years." The northern wind toyed with his graying hair.

I shivered and picked up my stainless-steel mug. My coffee was ice cold.

"So then no one else in your office tried to help you, I guess?" My voice grew more and more feeble with each word. What if I—no, what if Makoto had misunderstood everything and now he could never take it back?

"I had people on my side, who offered me encouragement, but there was no helping me, not really. Not up against the head of the company."

"Were all the executives who were arrested his allies?" I asked.

"I don't know if they were so much allies as they were lost too, each in their own little way. But considering their own positions, I suppose they probably couldn't oppose him. Meanwhile, more and more of the younger employees raised their voices and said that the CEO ought to be dismissed and the company completely restructured. I was in complete agreement. Once a company's fallen that low, your only way out is a full-scale revolution, essentially."

"So then, the reason you were so happy that night wasn't because you got promoted?" I asked.

"Oh no, it was," he assented, readily. "With a promotion, I'd finally be able to do some real work. My dream job, project development! The younger employees and I got carried away that night. We were so excited that we were finally going to be able to develop some serious, high-quality products. I felt like it had been touch and go for a bit there, but your old dad wasn't quite ready to give up the fight."

I was at a total loss for words by this point.

"So?" He puffed his chest out with a self-satisfied

smile. "I probably looked like a regular office worker to you, a boring old man stuck hanging on to a strap in a crammed rush-hour train every day. But I've had my fair share of drama, you know. Some of it's been good and some of it's been bad. And if there's one thing I can say for sure at this point, it's that the bad things will end. I know that sounds like a tidy little moral, but it's the truth. Just like how good things can't last forever, the bad stuff doesn't stick around that long, either."

He laughed out loud, sounding a little embarrassed. As if repelled by his cackling, the crows that had crowded around the picnic tarp with their sights set on our lunch leaped into the air all at once. The sound of flapping wings echoed around us while their black bodies were drawn into the deep blue of the sky.

I suddenly felt so alone that it made me dizzy.

The father had apparently intended his story to be encouraging, but unfortunately, I knew that there was one bad thing that had no end. Makoto's death wasn't going to be over one day. No matter how many years passed, how many decades, death was the one thing that definitely never ended. With this misunderstanding he could never take back still here in this world, Makoto would keep on being dead forever.

11

Mountain weather is unpredictable. After lunch, the sky suddenly grew dark, and the clouds thickened above us. I couldn't get back into sketching, no matter how I tried, so I finally went over to the father, who was still hanging his fishing line in the river.

"Let's go home."

We got stuck in a huge traffic jam that stretched out for around twenty kilometers on the toll highway, so the drive back felt like an eternity. Cars were bumper to bumper across three lanes. Every so often, we'd stagger forward like the cars were on the verge of collectively passing out, and then we'd stop again. Everyone was on edge, it seemed, and eventually, with no particular catalyst to set them off, drivers all around us leaned on their horns, the only possible act of resistance. But next to me, the father gripped the wheel without so much as a raised eyebrow. He was even humming along to the song that was playing.

Now that I was thinking about it, this was the first

time I'd seen his face so close up. He had the sort of round face that if you set up a panel of a hundred people, every single one of them would no doubt say he looked like a gentle man. Eyes that seemed to have never glared at anyone. And he might have been past forty now, but his skin was still firm and smooth. Despite everything he'd been through, there was no hint of the gloom that clouded Makoto's face.

"I want to ask you one thing," I said, almost whispering. "Does all that stuff in the past not matter so long as you're doing good now?" I wanted to understand. "You don't hold a grudge? You're not angry at the CEO and that boss? Can you really say you don't hate people anymore? I mean, they might still do some really terrible stuff to you. Maybe they're doing it already and you just don't know about it yet."

I was thinking of the mother.

The woman who had secretly cheated on him.

The woman he worshipped as his savior, full of powerful energy.

So maybe it wasn't only Makoto Kobayashi. Maybe every single person on this earth was just living their life under false impressions, misunderstanding other people and being misunderstood in turn. This was a heartbreakingly sad idea, but then there were also times when things went smoothly for just this reason.

"Oh, I held a grudge," he said, after a long silence. His face in profile, bathed in the headlights of the oncoming traffic, stiffened slightly. "Things might be going great now, but that doesn't make all those hard times go away. I can't get back those two years I spent like a zombie. I've never forgotten what my old boss did to me, and when the CEO was indicted, my first thought was, Ha, take that. Sometimes, I even got fed up with myself for thinking like this." He paused. "But all that stuff was blown right out of my head in an instant."

"An instant?" I looked at him curiously.

"That day, that moment."

"When?"

"You don't know?" The smile disappeared from his face. "It was the moment you came back to life."

"Oh." I felt a needle-sharp pain in my heart.

"After you took all those sleeping pills and you were on death's doorstep, I thought my own heart would stop first. I tried to hold it together somehow in front of your mother, but I was in an absolute panic inside. I called the ambulance as fast as I could, but once we got to the hospital, the doctor told us there was almost no hope, you were in a vegetative state at best. But even so, the doctors and nurses worked so hard on you, they really did everything they could. I was honestly struck by that. And then you miraculously came back to life, as if you couldn't help but respond to this passion of theirs. And I thought, for better or for worse, human beings are really something."

He spoke slowly, as if he was digesting the events of that day all over again.

"The joy I felt in that moment more than made up for every terrible thing that had happened to me up to that point."

I heard another horn from behind us. And then like a call and response, a horn blared up ahead and then to our right. I felt like running away, unable to sit in that seat any longer, and I craned my neck in the direction of each and every honk, my eyes racing around restlessly.

"It wasn't just me. That moment set the future in motion for someone else." The father's voice drew my gaze back to him. "I don't know if you noticed. But it was right after they saved your life in that hospital that Mitsuru began to say he wanted to be a doctor."

"Huh?" My jaw dropped.

"He said he's giving up on getting into medicine this year. I guess it was just all too sudden, and he won't be able to catch up in time for the scholarship exams. He's going to take a year off and really study hard so he can take them next year. He said we should send you to private school instead."

That *Mitsuru? No way. Impossible. Not a chance.* Although I tried desperately to deny it, somewhere in my heart

I knew it was true. I flopped back against the seat in resignation.

The truth was, I'd had a vague inkling that something was going on. Ever since I'd become Makoto Kobayashi—in other words, ever since Makoto's suicide—that sharp-tongued Mitsuru hadn't teased me once about my height.

"What do you want?"

It was already past nine by the time we got home. Mitsuru was apparently in his room; light was leaking out from the crack under the door. But I got no answer when I knocked, so I opened the door anyway.

He was studying at the desk in front of me. "Who said you could come in?" His voice was harsh as usual; his back remained turned to me.

"I just wanted to check on a couple things with you." I got straight to the point. "Did you decide to give up medical school this year because of me?"

"Spare me." He snorted. "I just didn't think I'd make it is all. I am your big brother. I'm not so great in the brain department, either." As always, the provoking tone and the little jab at me. "And when I checked into it, med school costs way more than I thought. I figured I'd get a job and earn my tuition once I started school, but I'd have a better shot betting on the scholarship exam next year. Change of plans, that's all. The end."

He turned back to his workbook.

"One more thing." I stopped him. "Is the reason you decided to become a doctor because of my suicide?"

"It's got nothing to do with you. It's because of your doctor," Mitsuru said, his voice flat. "I'd never seen a doctor working up close. I mean, they really do hold people's lives in their hands, and it was kind of amazing to see your doctor doing everything he could to keep you with us. And when I saw how insanely happy Mom and Dad were, it seemed like a pretty sweet gig. That's it. The patient coulda been anyone. Coulda been the person in the next room, coulda been a monkey even. The end."

He started to move his mechanical pencil again, but I stayed in the doorway.

"One more thing."

"You still got more?"

"Just one last thing."

"What the fuck do you want?"

"Really?"

"What?"

"Could it really have been a monkey?"

His pencil stopped. The sloping shoulders that so resembled Makoto's, the whorl of hair in the same position on the back of his head as Makoto's, all of it stopped moving for a moment.

"Think for two seconds, idiot!" Mitsuru whirled

around, his chair creaking, and the look on his face was so scary that I unconsciously shrank back.

"Think," he said again, glaring at me like he was trying to dig a hole in my head with his eyes. "The little brother who's been with me ever since I can remember, the weak, ugly, stupid, cowardly, deviant braggart who can't make friends so he follows me around everywhere I go, who needs to be rescued constantly, the kid I can't take my eyes off of, who I literally haven't been able to take my eyes off for fourteen years. For fourteen years. One morning, this kid, one totally normal and regular morning, he's suddenly dying right there in his bed. And he did it to himself. He made himself die. Think about what that would feel like!"

Once he'd said his piece, he lowered his voice abruptly and muttered, "The end," before turning back to his desk. He didn't look at me again, and the mechanical pencil racing across the pages of his workbook didn't stop again, either.

I stood there for a while like a batter who's struck out, until finally, at last, I turned on my heel and trudged back to my room.

I couldn't get to sleep that night.

The father's story. Mitsuru's story. There were more and more things I couldn't take back, things I couldn't undo, and suddenly, I felt so guilty about lying to my host family. It all tormented me. This day, today, the burden I was supposed to carry on Makoto's behalf was just too much. I was filled with such regret I could hardly stand it. The real Makoto should've heard the father's story today. I wanted the dead Makoto to hear Mitsuru's words.

I pressed my face into his pillow, and while I lay there wrapped in this regret that only I could understand, the inside of my nose twitched, and I felt something warm on my cheek.

It was then that a familiar voice came down from the ceiling. "Are you crying?"

Prapura. For the first time in ages. But right now, I just wanted him to leave me alone.

"It's not me," I said, muffled by the blankets. "These are Makoto's tears."

12

The idea of the Kobayashi family I'd had in my head gradually began to change color. It wasn't some simple change, like things that I thought were black were actually white. It was more like when I looked closely, things I thought were a single, uniform color were really made up of a bunch of different colors. That's maybe the best way to describe it.

Where there was black, there was also white.

Red and blue and yellow.

Bright colors, dark colors.

Beautiful ones and plain ones.

Depending on how you looked at it, you could see pretty much every color in there.

After we took our little trip to the river, I stopped avoiding the father. We had never been particularly close, so it wasn't like we were suddenly talking to each other nonstop. But we did manage to have the normal sort of conversation when our paths crossed. Mitsuru and I still fought all the time—no change there—but the way he talked to me so condescendingly didn't make me angry the way it used to. And when I thought about it, our fights were actually a pretty good way of blowing off some steam.

I was steadily finding my place in my host family, step by step. But my almost physical disgust with the mother's infidelity remained in my heart, an obstacle I just couldn't seem to clear.

I mean, everyone makes mistakes. After all, I'm only here myself because of a mistake in my past life. Getting all hung up what's already over and done is just stupid, to be honest.

I knew all that in my head, but I always got tense when I was actually face to face with the mother, strained. I felt like the father was honestly a really good guy and pretty gullible to boot, and lying to him was more than just uninspired, it was plain mean. And after swinging and missing with her infamous letter, the mom seemed like she had no other cards to play, so she quietly watched over me from a distance.

But the really annoying thing was while I was tied up with these feelings, I actually needed to talk to her about something sooner rather than later: the high school entrance exams.

The day of the exams was closing in, and yet we still

hadn't made a final decision about my school of choice. I kept insisting that I was only going to sit for the public school exam, and Makoto's parents kept pushing private school exams as a fallback plan. Mitsuru jumped in with his whole plan to get a scholarship to go to medical school so I should just apply for a single private school and not stress about the whole endeavor. We were never going to settle the matter like this.

I guess it was no wonder that everyone was worried, given my grades, and no one would want to have a kid doing a high school gap year in their family. But from my perspective, it was ludicrous to pay such a huge sum of money for a private school that I was only going to go to for five months.

The situation was just too complicated, and I'd been refusing to discuss this with the parents, but it was getting to the point where I was really going to have to just suck it up and talk to them.

Teacher, parents, student. The day was approaching when this dreadful combination was going to have to sit down and agree on the schools I was going to try for.

"Err, it's a bit late, but I've figured out the schedule for the parent-teacher conferences next week. Laugh, cry, whatever you want, but this is the last one of your junior high careers. So make sure your parents come."

Sawada announced the schedule during last homeroom on December 14, a Monday with the term-end exams in three days and winter break in ten.

"Each student gets fifteen minutes of interview time.
Whether that's long or short depends on you yourselves.
I put together the schedule using your student numbers,
basically, but we have three days for this, so let me know if
the time's bad for your parents. Okay, I'll call you up one
by one now, so come and get your time slot."

He looked around the classroom as he read out names
in a loud voice.

The printout I got just had "Day Two, 5:30 to 5:45"
scrawled on it in Sawada's handwriting. It was sure to be
a tough fifteen minutes, but, well, whatever. What concerned me more were Sawada's strange words when he
handed me the paper.

"Well, I've already talked plenty with your mom,
though, Kobayashi."

That was pretty much exactly what he said, one corner
of his mouth turning up in a smile. And then he saw the
baffled look I gave him and quickly changed the subject.

"Oh. Reminds me. Got a message for you from Mr.
Amano."

"Mr. Amano?" I frowned.

Sawada shrugged. "Said to show your face after school.
He's got something for you."

Colorful

"Okay." I cocked my head to one side, wondering what the something could have been.

Mr. Amano was the art club advisor, a quiet old guy who preferred to communicate with his brushes and storyboards rather than his mouth. But the advice he occasionally gave was spot on, and I secretly trusted him. I hadn't seen him since I stopped going to art club, though. What could he possibly have had to give me?

Puzzled, I stopped in at the prep room next to art club after school. Mr. Amano was basically always there. But that day, I knocked and knocked and still I got no answer. I couldn't hear anything inside, either. *He's probably in the teachers' room, then* . . .

I gave up and turned around. But I just couldn't. I didn't want to leave. I turned around again. I came full circle. My toes were once again pointed in the direction of the art room.

The scent of oil paints tickling my nose made me itchy. Like a man possessed, I passed the prep room and stood in front of the old familiar art room. I couldn't see any hint of a club member in the gloom beyond the frosted glass. Now that I was thinking about it, the school expressly prohibited students from attending club or sports practice in the period before exams. My heart suddenly got a whole lot lighter, and I opened the door to the art room in high spirits.

The moment I entered, I saw a strange sight in the supposedly empty room. I gasped in surprise.

The thick curtains kept the brick-red sunlight from shining in. A single easel, just one wooden easel, stood in the center of this deserted, cold room. There was a canvas sitting on it. As soon as I saw its blue surface, I knew it was my painting, the painting Makoto had started and I'd inherited. I was planning to take my time to finish it once the high school entrance exams were over.

A small silhouette stood motionless in front of it. A dark malice radiated from the silhouette, a tube of oil paint gripped in its right hand.

A tube without a cap, glistening inky black peeking out over the tip. The hand that held it slowly reached toward the canvas as if preparing to destroy this painting of ours with that black ink, and the face I could see in profile . . .

"Hiroka?" I called to her. *It can't be.*

The silhouette twitched and looked back at me.

It *was* Hiroka. Tube of paint still aimed squarely at the canvas, she looked at me, her eyes filled with a faint hatred.

"Why . . ."

Why would you do this to my painting?

I wanted to ask, but I couldn't actually speak. Her eyes were just so grim that I felt so incredibly sad.

In the evening gloom that blanketed the art room,

Hiroka was scared. In that moment, she was actually scared of her own self, radiating animosity and anger, toward what she didn't even know.

"It's okay." I was speaking before I even knew what I was going to say. "You can have the painting, Hiroka. You can do whatever you want with it."

In that moment, the seductive creature that had so bewitched me suddenly transformed into a little girl who was more fragile than anything else.

Hiroka dropped her eyes, all the fight running out of her. And then, without any warning, large tears were spilling out of those eyes. A glob of paint fell from the tube she clutched tightly and landed on the floor with a splat.

"It's weird. I'm weird. I'm losing my mind." She set the tube of paint on the easel and began crying, like a switch had been flipped. "I love beautiful things, I really do. But sometimes I just want to destroy them. I'm weird. I'm so weird."

I walked over to her and put my hands on her shaking shoulders. "That kind of stuff happens. It's not just you, Hiroka."

"I'm all messed up. My head's not on straight. I'm out of my mind. Everyone says so." She pressed her tearful face up against my chest.

"Everyone's messed up," I said, the truth I'd been through these last few months. "In this world, in the afterlife, whether you're a person or an angel or whoever, that's the norm. We're all normal and messed up."

"It's not just me?"

"It's not just you."

"It's not just me who gets mean?"

"It's not just you."

"It's not just me who wants to hurt someone?"

"It's not just you."

"There's this very nice Hiroka and then this very cruel Hiroka."

"Everyone's like that," I told her. "Everyone's got their own box of paints, and some of the colors are pretty and some are ugly."

Your bright colors always lit up Makoto's dark days, you know. It's too bad I wasn't able to tell her that.

Without realizing it, we're constantly saving someone and hurting someone else.

This world of ours is just so colorful that we can never decide on the right one, we never know which colors are real, which colors are our own.

"I want to have sex every three days, but then once a week, I want to join a convent. I want to buy new clothes once every ten days, an' I want new jewelry once every twenty days. I want to eat Kobe beef every day, an' I want to live a long time, but every other day I wish I could die. Am I really not messed up?" she asked, anxiously.

"Totally normal. Almost too ordinary," I said firmly, and added in a small voice, "But you should quit with the dying part."

Hiroka cried herself out—or at least that's what it seemed like to me—and was suddenly back to her usual baby-voiced self. She said something about how she was going to be late for a date and was about to leave the art room, but then stopped and turned around again.

"I can't take your painting. I just know I'll trash it one of these days. But you better finish it, every last bit of it. And then you have to take very good care of it forever, pinky promise?" she said with a smile, and then this time, she did leave.

She was a dizzyingly kaleidoscopic girl, so many colors in her, crying, laughing, suffering, tormenting. My interest in her only grew, not as a girl, but as this mysterious creature, and I felt a pang of regret that I only had this limited amount of time to watch over her.

I finally made it to the teachers' room after this lengthy detour and found Mr. Amano there.

"Oh, Kobayashi. Took you long enough," he said, his voice husky as ever, and held a large manila envelope out at me. "Here. What your mother asked me for."

Huh?

"I was going to ask Mr. Sawada to give it to you at the parent-teacher conference, but, well, I figured the sooner, the better with this sort of thing."

This sort of thing?

I accepted the envelope, with absolutely no clue to this "thing" he was talking about. It was thin and flopped over when I held it in one hand.

"I suppose you're having a tough go of it right now with all the studying, but once the entrance exams are over, come see us again. It just doesn't feel like art club when you're not there," he said, lowering his eyes, sheepishly.

I nodded, feeling sheepish myself, said my thanks, and left the teachers' room. I headed back to class on quick feet and opened the envelope the second I was back at my desk.

The "thing" that was inside was not a thing I ever expected to find.

13

When I came downstairs that night for supper with the envelope in question in one hand, the whole family was already sitting at the dining table, a rare evening when everyone was home. Father. Mother. Mitsuru. There was an unusual note of tension in each of their faces. They all turned as one to look at me.

"We have something serious to talk to you about, Makoto," the mother said, as if speaking for all of them.

"Yeah, I wanted to talk to you, too." I slowly held out the envelope. "This is from the art club advisor."

The expression on her face changed. The father and Mitsuru exchanged a meaningful look. So then, everyone besides me did know.

I handed the envelope to the mother and sat down next to Mitsuru. The smell of the cabbage rolls steaming before me on the table wafted up into my nose. They were gradually getting cold, and yet no one so much as picked up their chopsticks.

"I'm sorry if we crossed a line with this one." It was the

mother who broke the silence. "Your dad and I are going to leave the decision about high school up to you, Makoto. We just thought that before you make up your mind, you should know this is also an option you have. Of course, we want you to find a school where you can pass the exam, but we've also been wondering if there isn't a school you'd actually enjoy going to once you got in."

"I know," I said. "I get that much at least." The moment I opened the envelope, I knew she had only the best of intentions.

The few pages inside the envelope were copies of articles and documents about a particular high school. I'd heard of the place, too—an alternative school with special courses for art and music that used a credit selection system for the regular academic subjects. I'd greedily devoured the information on those pages and learned that I could choose a maximum of sixteen hours of art lessons a week if I went into the art program.

Of course, the school facilities were also something out of a dream. The art room in the photos was as big as a football field, and plaster busts for sketching were jammed in toward the back, like a herd of goats. The teachers were all famous, too, poached away from art universities, or else people who had taught in places like Paris and New York. On top of that, once a week, they invited practicing artists to speak in the lecture hall. They had really considered every last detail. A high percentage of their students went on to prestigious art schools or liberal arts universities, and as a result, the entrance and tuition fees were appropriately and absurdly high.

"It was Mitsuru who told us about this high school. We thought you might be happy if you could go to this kind of school."

I met Mitsuru's eyes, and he turned away silently.

"I had no idea about any of this," the mother confessed. "But from what I've heard, I feel like it would be just perfect for you, Makoto. So I gave Mr. Sawada a call."

Sawada had apparently explained to her that while the school itself was very competitive, its national academic T-score was not so high as all that. And for students applying to the art program, there was a practical exam in addition to the academic exam. This practical exam was considered the more important of the two, so Sawada said that I actually had a chance of getting in.

"And so then, the day before yesterday, your mom went out there and took a tour of the school," the father interjected, and the mother looked down, bashful.

"It's out on the outskirts of the city, but it is still in Tokyo," she said. "I wanted to check if it would even be possible for you to commute from our house. I didn't want to give you false hope, Makoto. And it *was* a little far, but not so far that you couldn't commute. It's about an hour by bus and train. And then you have to walk a little from the station to the school, but the area's so quiet and green. Just lovely."

The mother stood up and left for a moment before coming back with the thick school brochure in one hand and offering it to me. A gorgeous booklet, filled with colorful photographs. The cover showed the modern, silver-gray school.

"Looks great, doesn't it?" The mother turned eager eyes on me. "But I've learned only too well from all the courses and lessons I've taken that brochures are made by people who work for the places advertised, so they only ever talk about all the good parts. So I asked Mr. Sawada if there weren't some articles or something I could have a look at. He asked the art teacher and . . ."

I ended up with these pages delivered directly to me today.

"I wasn't trying to hide anything from you. I was planning to talk it over with you today when your dad and Mitsuru were here, too." She sounded excessively apologetic, a pleading edge to her voice. Maybe the look on my face was scary or something. But I wasn't angry.

Mother. Father. Mitsuru. Sawada. Mr. Amano. When I thought about how they had all been having this conversation and I'd been entirely in the dark about it, I didn't know how exactly to react to the whole thing. To be perfectly honest, I was . . . moved.

"Go to that high school, Makoto." Mitsuru looked right at me. "You're a dummy and a slowpoke and a useless coward, but the one thing you've always been good at is art. Go and paint your heart out at this school."

"Don't worry about the money." Now the father's eyes were on me, too. "I know I asked you to try for public school, but that wasn't so much about the money. It was more that I thought it might help you out to have some kind of goal to work toward. You just seemed so lost, heading nowhere in particular. I guess I wanted to see you working toward something instead. But if you're going to work for something, you should work for what you love."

"Mr. Sawada told me how the art club teacher is always saying such nice things about your paintings." Finally, it was the mother's turn to stare at me. "How he said that your skill was one thing, but the most important thing was how many fans you had. He said your paintings have a power to draw people in. I cried a little when I heard that." She was tearing up now, too.

I'd never cried out so hard, so deep in my heart, as I did in that moment with all of their eyes on me.

Makoto. You really did jump the gun.

It wasn't too late.

You rushed everything . . .

"Thanks," I muttered, my heart pounding, and my eyes dropped to the cover of the brochure once again.

The fresh green of the trees sheltering the grounds. The smiles on the students' faces as they walked to class in their stylish uniforms. The school itself, as massive as the Olympic stadium, rising up in the background.

"I was super surprised when I saw what was in the envelope Mr. Amano gave me," I said. "I knew high schools like this existed, but it wasn't like I could actually go to one, so I never bothered to check into it. I had no idea there was a school as great as this out there. I kept reading and I kept getting more and more excited. The more I learned, the more amazing it got. It's like some kind of paradise, you know? And I started thinking how great would it be if I could go to a school like this." I paused. "But I still want to go to a regular public high school."

"Why?" "How come?" "What's even in your head?" Mom, Dad, and Mitsuru blurted at the same time, and I tried to smile at them.

"It's just, I made a promise. To Saotome. We said we'd go to high school together."

"Saotome?"

"A friend from class."

"You're gonna pick a high school because of a thing like that?" Mitsuru burst out, angrily.

"It might be 'a thing like that,' but it's important to me," I told him. "He's the first friend I've ever had." I felt a lump in my throat, and even though I knew it was pathetic, I began to sob. "He's the first friend I've had."

The blurry veil of tears made the cover of the brochure shimmer and disappear. They could laugh and tell me it was totally stupid, but Saotome had told me about the 2,180-yen sneakers, and he was the most important thing in the world to me right now.

"The truth is, I think I was probably afraid. I wasn't refusing to take entrance exams. It was more like I didn't have the confidence to survive in high school."

Although I was still really upset and crying my eyes out, I kept trying to speak from my heart.

"I tripped up in junior high. I probably got off to a bad start. Everyone else took a step forward, but I just couldn't. Once I was late taking that first step, my rhythm got all messed up, and it made it even harder to move at all. Everyone in class kept pushing forward, leaving me behind, and my body got stiffer and stiffer until nothing was working at all anymore."

Right. That's probably how it went.

As I thought about Makoto's sorrow at being left behind, my voice got more and more hoarse.

"But some people stop and take a look back to check for you, like Saotome did. Maybe I'm just a simple guy, but

it made me so happy when he did. It's like, suddenly, I felt
I had a life. Like, I made friends with Saotome, so maybe
I'm a person who can make friends, just like everyone else.
Maybe I can make one friend at a time, bring them into
my life one by one. I started to feel like I might actually
be okay in high school. Even if I'm a little late taking that
first step again, I can catch up without getting lost and
panicking about it. Walking to school with a big group
of friends, messing around, taking a detour on the way
home—I want to do really simple things in high school.
That's it, totally normal stuff."

I wanted to give the real Makoto this extraordinary
average high school life. I wanted it from the bottom of
my heart, as I pressed my hands against my teary eyes.

Makoto's loneliness.

His fear.

His desires.

I knew them better than anyone else.

"Are you sure?" The father leaned forward. "I know
you love art. This is a chance to really go all in on it."

I nodded. "I'll join the art club in high school. I paint
because I love it. That's where I'm at right now. I haven't
thought any further ahead than that about committing to
art or making it into a career."

I felt bad for the mother after she'd gone all the way out
there to take a look at the school. But even if, hypothetically,

I did have a long future left to me, I figured it wouldn't be too late to start studying art as a major in university.

When I'd finished talking, silence fell around the dinner table. The only sound I could hear was the rattling of the windows in the wind and the *tic toc* of the clock carving out time. The mother, the father, and Mitsuru said nothing. They just sat and stared at me. But they didn't have to speak. I knew from those quiet gazes that they understood and accepted my decision.

"I'm starving." Mitsuru was the first to speak.

"Okay, let's eat. How about we all have a drink today?" the father suggested, a grin spreading across his round face. "You, too, Makoto. You're a grown-up now."

And so the matter of which high school I'd attend was settled. We agreed that I would try for public school like I decided, and just in case, I'd also take the exam for one private school as a backup. However they felt about the high school thing, though, the family seemed most pleased with the fact that I'd shared my feelings with them for the first time.

Of course, these were *my* feelings, not those of the real Makoto. At best, they were the feelings I imagined Makoto would have. The love the three of them were showering on me should have been directed at Makoto. It didn't belong to me.

Is it really okay like this?

Doubt started to really pick at me when I went back up to Makoto's room to study for the exams, after hanging out with the father for a bit while he had his dinner drink.

As my relationship with my host family got better, I grew more and more tangled up in these guilty thoughts. I wanted to go to high school in Makoto's place, I wanted to make friends, I wanted to paint. The stronger these desires got, the more I felt like I needed to apologize to the real Makoto. After all, right from the get-go, it was impossible for someone to waltz in and live someone else's life.

As long as I was me, the Kobayashi family would never know a real happy ending. All I could give them was a fake, a substitute joy. A fleeting one at that, with an expiration date.

Once I started thinking like this, I couldn't get anywhere with my studies, and if I tried going to bed, I wouldn't be able to sleep either.

Midnight. An in-between nowhere time.

To try to clear my mind, I headed down to the kitchen to make some coffee. When I walked by the living room, the lights were still shining brightly on the other side of the sliding door. So I stopped and casually peeked through the gap to find the mother's back still at the table.

"Oh!" She hurriedly swept something off the table to hide it in her lap when she noticed me. "Makoto, you're still up studying?" She looked flustered, like a student caught cheating.

Something was up. But whatever. I wasn't interested in what she was doing. I started to take a step forward and then abruptly changed my mind, took a step back, and popped my head into the living room.

"Sorry," I said.

"Hm?" She looked at me.

"I know you went to the trouble of getting that brochure and stuff for me."

She gaped for an instant and then smiled like a fog suddenly melting away. "It's fine. I never dreamed you were thinking things over this seriously. So I just went and stuck my nose in your business. I should be the one saying sorry."

With a wry smile, I set my feet in motion once more.

"Wait!" she called out from the other side of the sliding doors. "Could you come in for a minute?"

When I entered the room as requested and came to stand by her, she bashfully returned the thing she had hidden in her lap to the tabletop. It was a flimsy two-color pamphlet. The cover read, "You can do it, too! Fun and exciting finger puppet theater."

Fun and exciting finger puppet theater?

"Well . . . This woman I know runs a finger puppet troupe, and this is their pamphlet." The mother started to explain, looking extremely awkward. "I guess they volunteer to go around senior homes once a month. The other day, she asked me if I wanted to come join them. Of course, I said no at first. I'd only just decided I was going to dedicate my life to you boys. Not to mention that it's a rough period for you right now, what with the entrance exams and all. But she begged and pleaded, said they don't have anywhere near enough people right now. And looking at the pamphlet, I—well, I don't know how to put it . . . I don't know for sure, of course, but I started to get this feeling like maybe I was meant to be a finger puppeteer. It's strange."

I thought it was a whole lot stranger the way she went from zero to sixty like that, but I kept my mouth shut and my exasperation to myself.

"Honestly, I wonder why I'm like this." It seemed she was exasperated with herself, too. "I wonder if I'm still looking for that special something way down there in the bottom of my heart. I don't know what I could possibly hope to find now at my age, but I still can't stop looking. Aah, I'm so fed up with it myself. It's like a kind of greed or maybe just stubbornness."

Apparently, she *had* spent some time reflecting on

herself and her actions, but the way she didn't seem to actually process any of it was a blind spot of hers.

"It's not greedy or stubborn or anything." I'd been secretly thinking this for a while, and now I let it all out. "It's not such a big deal as all that. You just get bored really easily. That's it."

"What?" Her eyes widened as though this was real news to her. "I never thought about it like that." She was honestly astounded, and I could see her now not so much as a disgusting grown-up but actually more of an indiscriminate, capricious child. I had a hard time reconciling her with this new character, and I still couldn't shake the disgust I felt when I pictured her in the real with that flamenco teacher.

But maybe if I had more time.

A year, three years, five.

If the hours kept being stacked one on top of the other . . .

No, either way, that wasn't my part to play.

It was in that moment that I finally came to a decision about a certain something I'd been mulling over, something that had kept me scratching my head for a while, going in circles and coming to no real conclusions.

"So why don't you do the finger puppet thing?" I said, casually. "Just don't go quitting halfway through and causing trouble for everyone else."

"What?" She stared up at me. "You're okay with it?"

I shrugged. "It's none of my business. And I guess this is what Dad likes about you."

Her eyes shone, and I didn't forget to offer up a warning at the same time.

"Just don't lie to him anymore. A guy like that."

"You're right." The mother nodded, solemnly. "But for all that, your dad used to be quite the philanderer, you know."

"What?"

"Oh, this was before you boys were born. But on three separate occasions, his lovers came to me to ask me to leave him."

I was speechless. It goes without saying that I retreated in low spirits.

"Prapura." I ended up going back to my room without making coffee, and now I sat on the edge of the bed and called up to the ceiling. "Please come. I've got something important to talk about."

I was sure he would show himself now. I just got that feeling.

"So what's so important?"

Bingo.

Prapura popped into existence at my desk. In a beige suit, dressed to the nines as usual.

Colorful

"It's been a long time, huh?" I greeted the angel—or devil—sarcastically. "Any longer, and I would've forgotten what you look like."

"You just don't need a guide anymore," Prapura replied, smoothly. "You're familiar enough with your homestay family now. It's a good thing. I'm not your hairstylist, I'm not here for hair consultations, you know."

"What about serious consultations?"

"Depends on what it is," he sniffed.

"I want to give the real Makoto back to the people in this family," I said, calmly. My heart was certain now. "I want to give him back to them."

This was the end of the road for me. I did feel a twinge of regret, but this was the only way they were going to get their happy ending.

"I figured it was getting time for you to say that." The corners of his mouth slid briefly upward, but then he quickly grew serious again. "And there just might be a way to call back the soul of Makoto Kobayashi. You've been doing pretty well lately, and my boss is in top spirits. No one's really fussing over the details in this world, so he just might be open to the idea of a special exception. There's just one problem, however."

"And what's that?"

"You."

"Me?"

"You're in the way," Prapura announced, breezily. "In order for Makoto's soul to return to that body, yours would first have to leave it. And for you to leave it, you must remember the mistake you made in your past life."

"Oh!" I cried.

My mistake in my past life. Right, right, that was the rule here, wasn't it.

"I see you forgot about that." The angel glared at me. "Whatever. Just remember now. All the details. Get back to me with the mistake from your past life within the next twenty-four hours."

"The next twenty-four hours?"

"If you pass this little test, I'll bring it up with the boss for you. You return safely to the cycle of rebirth, Makoto Kobayashi's soul returns to that body. Hooray, huzzah, everyone's happy. But if you take even a single minute more than twenty-four hours, all your efforts will have been in vain. You'll never get another chance to call Makoto's soul back."

"Hang on a sec," I said, trying to push back the panic in my heart. "I'll try, I promise. I'll try, but . . . but why within twenty-four hours?"

"The number doesn't have any particular meaning. It's just more exciting with a time limit." He grinned.

"Exciting for who?" I glared at him.

"Me and my boss."

"Go to hell," I snapped, and dropped my head in my hands.

I glanced at the clock by my bed out of the corner of my eye—12:35 a.m. There was no way I was going to figure it out by this time tomorrow. I hadn't found so much as a vague hint after nearly four months of this.

"Don't go giving up before you've even started," Prapura said, his smile slightly restrained in the face of my despair. "Open your eyes. Really look. There are hints all over the place." He popped out of existence.

Hints all over the place?

14

Makoto's room. Ivory walls. Ceiling with a few spots here and there. The white light of the fluorescent bulb. The sky-blue rug reflecting this light.

South wall. Bay window and desk. I opened the drawers, but I couldn't find anything resembling a hint. The first drawer was full of pens and things. The second was notebooks. The third was a game console and a bunch of junk. Plus the porn.

East wall. Small bookshelf. Manga, a few art books by my favorite artists. Dictionary, textbooks, reference books. Fairy tales with faded covers made an appearance, too. Plus four thick photo albums. I flipped through the one to the far left, and there was a little Makoto, his smiling face cherubic. He was so tiny and surprisingly cute. He didn't know yet that he was fated to be tiny forever.

Northeastern corner. A dresser of light pinewood. The clothes inside were neatly sorted. Shabby street wear in the top drawer. The farther down the dresser, the newer the clothes got. The very bottom drawer even had a red shirt tucked away inside with the price tag still attached. Maybe he wanted to change his image, but in the end, this was just too flashy for him.

North wall. Completely taken up by the bed. And underneath this, the secret boots slept in secret. I knew I would never wear them, but I wasn't quite ready to let go. Could the secret boots have been a hint? Probably not.

"Open your eyes. Really look."

But I don't know. I can't find any hints.

There was no furniture on the west wall, just the door that led out and down the stairs. In the end, I was forced to go out that door and start the next day without getting a wink of sleep. I'd never before welcomed so impatiently the widening circle of pale light of the sun rising.

Seventeen hours until time was up.

I dragged myself downstairs, heavy and slow after the inadvertent all-nighter, and was greeted by the delicious scent of miso soup wafting out from the kitchen.

"Oh!" The mother flashed me a bright look. "Good morning!" In contrast with my own haggard face, her cheerful smile was far too fresh. As she stirred the miso soup with one hand, she bent and straightened the index finger of her other hand. *One, two, one, two.* "Hee hee! I've already started my finger puppet training."

A vital woman indeed. Scratching my head, I headed for the washroom.

Bathroom business. Wash face. Change clothes. Breakfast. Brush teeth. Comb hair. I performed my routine in the usual order with more care than usual. Laser-focused, I made careful note of everything, from the seat of the toilet to the bristles on my toothbrush. And the pale peach soap. Plus the glistening fried egg I had for breakfast. Even the ingredients in the hair mousse I'd finally figured out how to use without drowning my head in the stuff.

And yet I didn't know. I couldn't find any hints.

Eventually, I left the house with nothing to show for my efforts and headed toward school. I walked slowly enough that the twenty-minute walk took half an hour. It was the same old town as ever, and no matter how hard I stared, it was still nothing more than the same old town as ever. The morning breeze was brisk and cool, and heavy clouds hung over the sky, which quickly put me in a despairing mood. And again, I arrived at school with nothing to show for my efforts.

Fifteen hours until time up.

First period was gym, and soccer on top of that. I hated soccer. Whenever someone bigger came at me during a scrimmage, my tiny self would instinctively shrink back and try to get out of the way.

Colorful

"You have to stand your ground, Kobayashi!" Sawada ripped into me once again that day. "Don't just slink away like some kind of petty thief!"

A bolt of electricity shot through my body, like I'd been hit dead on by a bazooka. In an instant, the ground, the sky, the world shattered, and I saw it so clearly in my mind: me in a ski mask, carrying a sack over my shoulder, skulking across the low rooftops. *Yes. Right.* I slammed my fist into the ground and shouted, "Past-life me was some kind of petty thief!"

Of course, nothing so fantastical as this actually happened. The soccer game ended with nothing bigger than Sawada yelling at me. Naturally.

It was the same in all my other classes. And why not? There was no reason anything special would happen today of all days. About all I could do was narrow my eyes and take a fresh, painstaking look at every minute and every second of this utterly average day. But no hint of any kind revealed itself to me, and in the blink of an eye, it was time for lunch.

"What's up with you today?" Saotome asked, a worried look on his face, as I sat lifeless in a seat by the window after we finished eating. "Your eyes are deadly. You tired?"

"Didn't get enough sleep." I showed him my bloodshot eyes.

"Whoa! You're really giving it, huh? Studying all

179

night?" Saotome misinterpreted my all-nighter in a good way. "I gotta get in there, too. We'll be in real trouble if one of us fails. We gotta both pass."

I felt an awkward joy and a slight confidence boost at how gently, artlessly he was offering these words to me. To be honest, it kind of made me not want to let go of Makoto's body. *I really do want to go to high school with Saotome,* I thought, somberly.

I was also worried about Makoto. Would he be able to keep things up with Saotome if he did manage to make it safely back to this body? Would he cherish the friend I'd gone to the trouble of making? I had every intention of passing the baton with a please and thank-you, but given Makoto's personality, I couldn't help but feel a bit nervous.

"Saotome?" I decided to lay the groundwork anew. "If . . . This is just an if, but if tomorrow, I went back to being the old me, all gloomy and quiet and hard to get a read on, could you maybe not just walk away? Maybe don't judge me right away, just keep an eye on me for a while?"

"Huh?" He looked perplexed, which was understandable. "What're you on about? You planning to do that or something?"

"I don't know yet," I started to explain, awkwardly. "It's like I'm still emotionally unstable, you just don't know what'll happen and all."

Colorful

Saotome hummed thoughtfully as he sat down in front of me, rested his chin on the seat back, and set himself to considering the situation.

The classroom was quiet now that the lunch servers had left, and we were the only ones still in there. In contrast with this stillness, the field outside the window was really lively. A few groups playing soccer, and even more trying their hand at volleyball. Countless balls danced up toward the heavens, below a sky that was gray like watered-down ink.

"When I was in elementary school, okay?" Saotome said. He had also turned his gaze out the window. "I've always been the type who can get along with pretty much anyone. But there used to be just this one kid I was no good with. We were in the same friend group, and he was the only one I had trouble talking to. Whenever it was just the two of us, we'd sit there in silence. It was super awkward. It looked like he was avoiding being alone with me, too, so I figured he just hated me. But one day, after school, when we all stayed to play outside, right? We had a great time. Just talking all cool and busting a gut at each other. And like, I was totally thrilled. It's all good now, no more problems. We'll be pals from now on. The next morning, I went to school all excited, and he'd turned back into that awkward guy again."

Saotome laughed, briefly.

"My kid brain suddenly realized, today and tomorrow are completely different. Tomorrow isn't a continuation of today."

I nodded, silently. Less out of agreement than to share his sadness.

"If you go back to being the old Kobayashi tomorrow and get all weirdly on guard the instant I come near you, I think I'll react the same way. I'd probably be pretty sad, you know," he said. "But you did give me a kind of heads-up here. I guess I could keep an eye on you and see where it goes." His face suddenly scrunched up, and he burst out laughing.

My heart was so full that all I could do was give him a simple "Thanks" in return.

Not five thousand years ago, not five thousand years from now. I'm glad I got to meet Saotome now.

But, of course, unless I could remember my mistake from my past life, the real Makoto wouldn't return to this body and my laying the groundwork with Saotome would have been for nothing.

In the afternoon, I was spurred on by a sense of urgency as the sky above grew increasingly grim. Despite my many efforts, no matter how I focused the lenses of both eyes to the microscopic level to examine every single thing

I came across, I still hadn't found anything along the lines of a hint at school. That said, I didn't expect I'd find anything in the Kobayashi house either if I went home, not after I'd already searched it so thoroughly.

Just over nine hours until time was up.

I prowled the school after classes were done, desperately hoping to come across even a hint of a hint. It was right before exams, so there wasn't a soul in the large building, and the place had the unbroken silence of a movie theater after closing time. Thunder started to grumble in the distant sky, shaking the hushed air. But even when the sound of rain joined this rumbling, I didn't have the mental bandwidth to bother with the weather. I kept walking and looking, stopping, staring hard at random objects, and then starting out again.

The gym. The storeroom. The janitors' closet. The meeting room. The audiovisual room. The broadcast room. The boys' bathrooms. Shop. Home economics. The laboratory. The music room. I checked everywhere I could. Finally, there was only one room left.

A room filled with my own memories, even though I'd only spent a brief period of time in it. The art room.

If there was going to be any kind of hint in this school, it would be there. I was secretly sure of it. Which is exactly why I was sort of scared and had put it off to the very last.

Lightning flashed through the hallway windows, and

bathed in that light, I put one foot in front of the other, slowly moving toward the art room. The smoky gloom inside the school further heightened my anxiety. Would I be able to dig up a hint in the place that had been a shelter for both Makoto and me? If I failed, I wouldn't get a second chance to bring Makoto's soul back.

Boom! I'd just put my hand on the door to the art room when I heard the roar of a lightning strike somewhere. I felt the shock of it like the floor was sinking beneath my feet.

A heartbeat later, I heard a girl shrieking inside the pitch-black art room. "Eeaah!"

I flew inside, whirling my head around for the source of the cry. But the room was blanketed in darkness; my eyes were useless. It was only when I turned on the lights that I finally saw the figure of a girl crouched under the teacher's desk.

Blinking furiously at the sudden glare, the girl gasped when she noticed me and visibly relaxed. "Kobayashi . . ."

It was Shoko.

"Oh!" My heart skipped a beat. This was the first time I'd come face to face with her since that day. "Wh-what? Why are you in here?" I stammered.

"Charcoal sketching," she said, weakly.

"Sketching?"

"And then the lightning suddenly . . ." She poked her face out from under the desk, ever so timidly.

When our eyes met, we both looked away at the same time.

"You're sketching in the dark?" I asked.

"Yeah." She nodded. "I wanted to draw."

"At least turn on the lights."

"If the teachers caught me, they'd get mad." She turned away from me, her voice cold.

A flash of silver light illuminated her face in profile.

"Aaaaah!" she screamed, and dived back under the desk. Even after the lightning had subsided, she kept her head tucked firmly into herself.

"Are you okay?" I didn't really have much choice in the matter now, so I walked over to the desk. "If you're that scared, go home already. You can't draw like this anyway. I can stick with you until your house."

This kindness, of course, came from the guilt I felt, but she apparently hadn't forgotten about that day. She kept her mouth shut and her back turned to me.

"I'm sorry about the other day. I won't try anything today. Don't worry."

I was trying extra hard to be nice, but the only response I got from under the desk was a puff of white breath. She was as stubborn as always.

"C'mon, let's go," I urged her.

Silence.

"You gonna stay here forever?"

Nothing.

"The lightning's not stopping, you know."

Crickets.

"I feel like there'll be another hit in thirty seconds."

Zip.

Thirty seconds passed, and I finally got annoyed. "Go and get hit by a bolt of lightning, then." With this child-ish parting remark, I turned my back on her. I'd forgot-ten why I'd even come to the art room at that point, so I stomped back out into the hallway. I really was no good with that girl.

"I . . ." Shoko said, when I had taken a step out of the classroom. "It's not like I was thinking about you like you were the Little Prince or anything, you know!"

Her voice carried well. When I looked back, she was standing angrily in front of the desk.

"I mean, I never thought you were cool or whatever."

For some reason, my heart throbbed at those eyes, a puppy ready for a fight.

"You're nowhere near a prince. You're basically a peas-ant. I totally knew you were pathetic, too, Kobayashi. I was always watching your sad self, okay? When we were in seventh grade, the other boys in class were bullying you, right? I know. I mean, I was always watching you, after all. Always. And back then, I was being picked on, too, in the class next door."

Her voice grew indistinct against the increasingly violent pounding of the falling rain. I slowly moved back toward her so I could hear her better.

"I've always been on the outside, ever since I started at this school. Everything was just so different from elementary. Everyone looked so stylish and mature. I had a really hard time trying to keep up with my new friends. They used to tell me all the time that I was too slow. That just being with me was annoying. And I'd say, like, what do you mean, and they'd be all, you're so sticky. They began to ignore me or hide my slippers and stuff, but I absolutely refused to cry. When I didn't cry, they'd tell me how useless I was and pick on me even more . . . You used to get chased around in the hallway a lot back then, too, Kobayashi. A whole bunch of guys'd surround you and try out wrestling moves on you. They'd yank your pants down. You were their little toy. How could I possibly think that you were cool or anything like that?"

She laughed briefly, and then got serious again.

"But you didn't cry, either, so I kind of figured we were in the same boat."

I couldn't stand it. I dropped my eyes to the floor. She looked like she was about to burst into tears, but still she absolutely refused to cry, and the sight hurt my heart unexpectedly.

"It wasn't just that you didn't cry. You seemed way more fine with it than I ever was. You always just sat there and endured it, no expression on your face, your eyes quiet. Like a plant waiting for the storm to pass, you know? I always wondered how you could just take it like that. I figured there had to be something. So I just kept my eyes on you. I was watching you. And then one day, I followed you after school and ended up in the art room."

I looked up again, and Shoko lowered her eyes as though remembering the moment.

"When I saw you painting, I sort of got it. Like, oh, right. Kobayashi's got this whole world all to himself. It was so deep, so clear, I was sure it had to be safe there. I was jealous. I wanted a world like that too, so I went ahead and joined the art club right then and there."

I stared at her. "That's how you joined the art club?"

"Yeah." She nodded. "And ever since, I've been trying to be like you, Kobayashi. Standing beside you, I watched and learned, I painted, I looked for my own place. I wanted that kind of strong world, where so long as I had that, I could get through anything without crying, without getting upset. But it turns out I'm not a great painter. I couldn't manage anything decent, so it wasn't much of a world at all."

Shoko stuck the tip of her tongue out.

"But even still, I felt peaceful somehow when I was painting. On bad days, I'd come to the art room after school and flush all those sad feelings away. Painting made me feel like I could come back to school again tomorrow."

It was chilly alone together in the art room. The wind snuck in through a crack somewhere to make the plaster busts near the window clatter and rattle. And then lightning raced through the sky again. But Shoko didn't scream this time; she simply braced herself and kept talking.

"I was so happy when we ended up in the same class this year, Kobayashi. And yeah, sure, maybe I did build you up a bit in my mind. I always get these ideas and then run with them, so I probably did make up the parts of you that I wanted to see. But even so, you are special, okay? You've got a whole world of your own, unlike everyone else. This world was really pushing me over the edge, and then you showed me there was another one on the other side of the canvas. And then *that* Kobayashi—"

"He was gone for a long time," I said, feeling apologetic. "And when he came back to school one morning, he suddenly seemed totally different."

Shoko offered a wry smile in response. "I was honestly so surprised. You were absent for soooo long, and then when you finally came back, you were part of this world all of a sudden. That other world inside you was gone. You were so incredibly normal. Or like, not normal—you were just like all the other boys. I freaked out. It was such a shock. And it made me feel kind of lonely."

"Sorry . . ." Belatedly, I was filled with regret for all the terrible things I'd said to her. Makoto hadn't been a fictional character for her. He'd been something like a guide, a person who somehow made the harsh reality of this world a little easier to handle. I was ashamed that I'd been such a prisoner of Makoto's wounds that I'd been totally indifferent to everyone else's.

It wasn't just Makoto.

And it wasn't just Shoko or Hiroka, either.

Anyone and everyone in this terrible world was broken in their own way.

"But I'm okay with it now." Her voice was bright now, clear, crisp, excited. "I get it. I've been thinking a lot about the things you said to me that day, and this time for sure, I get it."

"Get what?" I frowned.

"You didn't *change*, Kobayashi. You just went back to being who you always were."

"Who I always was?"

"Exactly. You started off being a boy from this world, you know? A regular kid just like everyone else. But then me and everyone else went and locked you up in that other world. And maybe it was easier for you to be over there, anyway. Who knows? But then, suddenly—I don't know what happened, but you made it back to this world. You managed to get back to being who you always were." She jerked her chin up and grinned. "Congratulations, Makoto Kobayashi."

Out of the blue, I was overcome with this strange sensation, like I'd just realized everything I knew was a lie, like I'd been buttoning up my shirt all wrong my whole life. Something was bothering me. Shoko had her own weird ideas and was running off with them like always, but I couldn't help but feel like there was something more hiding in her words now.

"The old Kobayashi was pretty good, but I think the new Kobayashi's not too bad, either. You're way ruder than before, and you're mean sometimes, but that actually makes you easier to talk to. And I feel like you're really alive now." She tilted her head back and looked up at the ceiling. "And to be honest, I knew. I knew you were still the same deep down, even if you'd changed a lot. It was just that I wanted you to be the old Kobayashi, the one who was convenient for me. But the truth is, I really did know that the Kobayashi in that world and the Kobayashi in this world were different, but also the same."

"How?" My heart started racing. "How did you know that?"

"I mean, that picture you're painting didn't change, so." She shrugged.

"Picture?"

"Yeah, your painting," she replied. "The unique way you use color. The touch of your brush, the way you look at the canvas. That's how I knew you were still you."

Instantly, everything I could see began to radiate with a vivid splendor. I slowly lifted my face and looked around the classroom with fresh eyes.

The eggshell color on the walls that had warmth even in winter. The burnt-umber shelves that occupied the rear of the classroom. The indigo curtains framing the dark windows. The forest green of the blackboard at the front of the room. The burnished silver of the easels. The porcelain skin of the plaster busts. The chestnut beret someone had set on one of their inert heads. The floor stained with multicolored blobs of paint. The white gleam of the fluorescent lights hidden under their dusty covers. Shoko's black hair shining in the hazy glow. *There are hints all over the place.* There actually *were* hints all over the place.

I turned my eyes back to Shoko. There was a smudge of charcoal on her cheek, maybe from when she'd been sketching. I reached out and gently wiped it away with a finger. She flinched and stiffened for an instant, and I was overcome with the urge to hug her, but I restrained myself.

Colorful

The shrimp who hadn't even been in Makoto Kobayashi's field of view. This girl had saved Makoto
Kobayashi.

"Wait here," I said, grabbing her shoulders. "I'll be
back in a minute, so just wait here."

"Where are you going?" she asked, baffled.

"Doesn't matter," I insisted. "Just wait. I'll walk you
home after."

"I guess." She looked up at me, doubtfully. "Fine."

"Okay? Make sure you wait. Promise."

I flew out of the classroom and raced up the stairs,
looking for a place where I could be alone. I was exuber-
ant, too excited for words. I opened the door that led from
the landing to the roof and saw that the rain was slowing
already. And the thunder and lightning had stopped.

The flash of light I saw was inside my own head.

15

The misty, silky rain quietly painted a slick coating on the concrete roof. The clouds were still thick in the sky, and darkness enveloped me like night had already fallen. When I looked down, the ground below was swallowed up by the same inky black.

Shivering in the cold drizzle in the gap between dark and darkness, I waited for him to come. He had to come. No doubt with frilly white parasol in hand and a smirk on his face.

Eventually, I heard the clacking of footsteps behind me and looked back to see Prapura standing there, a smirk on his face and frilly white parasol open above his head.

"I've said this any number of times already," Prapura said when our eyes met, and held the parasol higher. "Issued by the boss. This umbrella, not my style."

"I know," I said with a laugh. "I know what my mistake was."

Prapura nodded, quietly, and we stared at each other through the veil of rain between us. As I looked into his lapis lazuli eyes, my racing heart slowed, and I felt strangely calm somehow.

"I committed a murder, right?"

The look on the angel's face didn't change.

"I killed someone."

Still, he waited.

"I killed myself."

Prapura's gaze on me was steady.

"I murdered my own self," I said, biting my lip hard. "I'm the soul of the Makoto Kobayashi who committed suicide."

Prapura tossed his pearly umbrella high up into the sky. "Ding ding ding!"

16

The darkness of heaven and earth instantly became light. It was so dazzlingly bright that I nearly fainted. I felt like my physical body was spinning around and around and around and around, and yet I was still curiously composed as it all came back to me.

Me before the suicide. The memories I'd lost. Makoto Kobayashi's fourteen years . . .

I'd always loved drawing, ever since I could remember. At the same time, I also loved playing outside with my friends when I was little. Although I did have this shy and timid side, I was extremely popular thanks to the fact that I had one thing I excelled at. Up until grade three or four, the kids in class would crowd around my desk at every break, and I would draw manga or game characters on the scraps of paper they held out. Thinking about it now, it was a golden age. I was very blessed.

But the sun started to set in the last couple years of elementary school. My classmates were more grown-up now; they didn't want my childish drawings anymore.

Colorful

Some of them even gave me back the pictures politely, like "I'm done with this, thanks." But still, I felt like they were saying they were done with me. I lost sight of my own value. On top of that, I wasn't growing as much as I thought I would, and my shorter friends shot past me one after the other. I was like a pop star gradually dropping down the charts.

I hit rock bottom in grade seven. Right when I first started junior high, there was a group that always hung out together, and whenever I said anything, this one guy would say, "Gross." He deliberately said it loudly enough for everyone else to hear. In time, the rest of the group started to copy him—"Gross, gross." I'd never been the talkative type to begin with, and this just made me hold my tongue even more. It was only a matter of time before the bullying started. And then it did. And I still didn't want to remember that part of my life, even if it was all in the past now.

My only salvation was my family and art club.

Mitsuru was a jerk, but my parents doted on me to the point of excess. My slightly unstable mother, and my smiling, peaceful father. Just being with them made me breathe a sigh of relief.

At art club, I could forget about everything else and immerse myself in my beloved painting. Maybe I painted so that I had something to lose myself in and forget the outside world. A little recess for my heart. A meaningful escape. Deflected passion. I totally hadn't noticed that Shoko had been watching me that whole time.

The bullying let up when I went into eighth grade, but I stuck out like a sore thumb in my new class. I deliberately kept to myself. I was afraid someone would say "gross" if I said something accidentally, and that this would trigger a new round of bullying. No one could stop it. No one could save me. I couldn't rely on anyone. I couldn't trust them.

I locked myself up in my own little world. I painted more and more pictures of gloomy darkness, full of cold colors. Even *I* thought I was kind of in a bad place.

If only I could have just lived in my own little world, everything would have been fine. But maybe deep down inside, I was looking for something more than that. I got more and more anxious. I even started throwing up for reasons unknown around the start of ninth grade. My parents were worrywarts, so I didn't tell them any of this, though. But out of the blue, I'd be overcome with nausea; I was constantly in the bathroom throwing up. I had a hunch that this wasn't a physical problem, but some kind of mental issue, which just made it all that much more disturbing.

I can't go on like this, I thought, seriously. I don't think I can go on like this. I have to do something.

But what?

Colorful

I decided to try painting a bright picture.

I had a flash of an almost transparent blue, the color of the rolling ocean. The figure of a horseman heading up to the surface from the deep, dark seafloor.

I began to paint as though in a trance. As I worked, I promised myself that once this piece was finished, I would try to pull free of my own deep, dark place.

But before that could happen, the absolute worst day came along. Hiroka. Mom. Dad. They had been my salvation, and now they came to beat me down one after the other. Their blows hit all the harder because I'd been so close to turning myself around. The world plunged into darkness, and I couldn't see color at all anymore. My depression and vomiting got worse, I stopped being able to think properly, my head felt like it was always full of cotton.

This was when the word *death* started to take on a strange reality. It had flitted through the back of my mind every so often since seventh grade, but it was more than a passing thought now.

Maybe I could just die.

The idea came to me sudden and serious one day. And once it did, it wouldn't leave my head. It was far easier to think about dying than living, and death was more appealing than life at that point.

My mom struggled with insomnia, and a relative had once bought her some sleeping pills overseas. But my dad said she was better off not taking them and tucked them away. I remembered exactly where he had put them, and I secretly pulled them from their hiding place in the middle of the night.

It just felt so natural to swallow the bottle of pills. And then I died.

Or I should have.

But then a strange angel popped up in front of my wandering soul . . .

"Congratulations! You've won the lottery! Your do-over has been a marvelous success!"

The wave of memories receded, and when I suddenly came to with a gasp, I was back in that same gap between the world above and the world below.

This time, though, I had a proper flesh-and-blood body, and in front of me, Prapura's own body was wrapped in white cloth, the folded wings on his back exposed. I hadn't seen this formal angel dress of his in a while. He was also back to his old polite way of speaking.

"I do believe you have come to understand the situation on your own, but allow me to explain," Prapura began.

"The homestay is not simply disciplined training for the soul. It is instead a test period to see whether or not a soul that has abandoned itself as yours did is able to return to the self once more. Put another way, it's a spiritual test drive. Which makes it only natural that the homestay placement be your very own household. You souls review your own problems again in the very place where you foundered. So? What do you think? Makes a fair bit of sense, doesn't it? But it wouldn't be the least bit interesting if we told you all this from the outset, so I kept that part to myself," he informed me, shamelessly.

My shoulders slumped. What could I say to this angel? When I thought about it, so much of what Prapura said and did had been questionable right from day one.

"So like, looking back, okay?" I finally said. "Your guidance was so half-assed. You always left out the important bits. I feel like I suffered a lot more than I actually needed to. But I guess that was on purpose?"

"Of course." The angel thrust his chest out. "You may have won the lottery, but we're giving you the chance to live here after you've already died once. We really must have you put in the appropriate amount of effort. You can't return to life simply because you're lucky with lotteries."

"But you *made* me win the lottery. You tricked me. You even forced me to work," I complained.

"And as a consequence, you will be able to live once more as Makoto Kobayashi, which you are secretly grateful for. We get results."

I let out a sigh. I'd never beat this weird angel.

He was right, though; I was glad I wouldn't be removed from the cycle of rebirth, disappearing like the bubbles in a glass of soda, with all those dark feelings of four months earlier in my heart; without clearing up all those mis-understandings, without knowing how my suicide would affect my family, without having met Saotome, without having held a sobbing Hiroka, and without even noticing the existence of Shoko, the person who had saved me in the end. I was secretly overwhelmed by all this emotion.

"Why can't you simply let all that emotion out, then?" Prapura asked, opening up his hands in front of him.

I thought for a bit and then said, "First of all, that's not the kind of person I am."

"I see."

"Second, I'm confused by this sudden development."

"Oh-ho!"

"Third, I hate that you tricked me."

"Heh-heh!"

"And finally . . ."

"Finally?"

"I'm scared," I muttered, and yanked my chin up to stare at him. "What's going to happen to me now?"

"Happen? You're going to live on as Makoto Kobayashi. That's all." Prapura's answer was plain and simple.

"And what are you going to do?"

"I'll witness the next lottery and accompany the win-ning soul."

"So you're finished as my guide?" I asked.

"You don't need a guide anymore."

"Don't I?"

"I don't believe so." Prapura flapped the wings on his back as if to insist upon the point. As I watched them move, I felt a sudden courage in my heart—no, of course I didn't. I still felt uncertain, unclear.

"A second ago, before we came here, I remembered everything from before the suicide. And it kind of made me lose confidence in myself again," I confessed.

"Confidence?"

"Can I really make it work down there?"

"Why wouldn't you be able to?" Prapura frowned. "Haven't you done quite well on your second chance?"

"It's just, it was someone else's business then."

That's right. During the do-over, Makoto Kobayashi had been a total stranger, nothing more than a place to live temporarily. That's why I'd been able to act without over-thinking every little thing. I hadn't cared what happened next. I cheerfully withdrew my savings, bought whatever happened to catch my eye, said whatever I wanted to whoever I liked.

"But I can't do that when it's actually me. I get all cautious. And anxious. And cheap, too, y'know?"

As proof of this, I was starting to regret that I'd blown so much money on sneakers—28,000 yen! I was already beating myself up about it.

Prapura let his wings rest and stared at me. His deep blue eyes were clear today again, not a cloud in the sky. Those eyes had lied to me, gotten mad at me, teased me, but still always watched over me somehow nevertheless.

"You can simply think of it as a homestay."

"A homestay?" I frowned.

"Exactly." The angel nodded. "You'll spend a while in the world below again, and then you'll come back here. A human life is a few decades at best. Think of this in a more lighthearted way. Tell yourself you're merely starting another, slightly longer homestay."

A few decades at best. A longish homestay. It *would* be easier if I thought about it like that.

"There are no rules for a homestay. People are welcome to spend their time however they wish with the family they are given. However, you cannot leave the homestay early."

"Right," I interjected. "You can't quit, can you?"

Prapura raised an eyebrow. "Did you want to withdraw?"

I didn't answer. When all was said and done, I did actually want to go back to that world one more time.

He nodded, as if he could see right into my heart.

"If in the world below, you do end up wanting to curl into yourself once more, please remember this time you spent on your do-over. Remember how it felt to move

freely without trapping yourself in your own expectations.
And remember the people who helped you up."

As I stared down at my feet wordlessly, I reflected on
the fleeting four months of my do-over. I'd spent time with
all kinds of people, done so many things with them. I got
the feeling that I would never have made it back to myself if
even one of them hadn't been there for me.

"Now it's getting to be about time for you to return to
the world below," Prapura said, as if announcing the train's
arrival at its final station. "Shoko is still in the art room, and
she's starting to worry that you're not coming back."

Oh, right, I remembered. I'd left Shoko hanging in that
cold art room.

"Your family is waiting at home. They are discussing
what they should get you for your birthday. It's two weeks
from now, after all."

I nodded.

"You must hurry back there and study so you can pass
the exam for the same high school as Saotome."

I nodded.

"Hiroka is waiting for you to complete the blue
painting."

I nodded.

"You need to exist in that world."

I nodded. I had to be in that world. Behind my closed

eyelids, I pictured this world where people were waiting for me.

A world so colorful it made me dizzy sometimes.

I was going back to that vortex of brilliant hues.

Time to live, drenched in color with everyone else.

Even if I didn't know what exactly it was all for.

"Thanks, Prapura." I turned back to the angel. "I won't forget you."

"Nor will I forget you," he said, with his usual poker face. "You were a handful."

"You were the first person I could really talk to."

"Now then, I will begin my final job as your guide."

"It's weird. I could honestly talk to you about anything."

"To guide your return to the lower world. Please do as I say."

"I felt so comfortable hanging out with you."

"First, please close your mouth and concentrate."

"Probably because you're an angel."

"Please close your mouth."

"You're not a human being. You don't hurt people, you don't get hurt so easily. I guess that's why I felt so comfortable."

"I told you to shut it!"

A sudden whack on the head startled me into silence.

"Ow," I groaned, and looked up to see Prapura glaring at me with his familiar lower-world-mode scowl.

Colorful

"How long do you plan on rambling on here? Just do what I tell you and go home already. I mean, I've got to get to the next lottery."

This was much more Prapura's style. And for all his rough words, his lapis lazuli eyes were tinged with a little—just a little—sadness. I was plenty satisfied with that.

"First, close your eyes tight."

I closed my eyes tight. Warm tears spilled over the edges.

"Take a deep breath."

I took a deep breath. My throat closed up, my heart hurt.

"Focus on going home and take a step forward. That will allow you to return to your world. Adieu, Makoto Kobayashi. Live strong."

"Bye, Prapura."

I took my first step to go back to my world.

AFTERWORD

When a dead spirit wins the lottery, they're given the chance to return to the world and live life over again in someone else's body. This idea for a novel came to my head more than twenty years ago. Like a bud rapidly opening into a flower, this story bloomed in my brain, and I desperately chased after it to write the book. And from the moment it was released, *Colorful* has been blessed with so many wonderful encounters and has transformed into one new shape after another, continuing to expand and grow: it is now a film adaptation, a stage play, an anime, a manga, and much more. Now, at last, it has crossed the Pacific Ocean to be published in the United States—and anticipation of new encounters grows and unfurls in my heart.

I want to write a novel that will allow young people who are tired of living to have a break from their own lives. This thought was the starting point for the whole endeavor.

Teenagers in Japan have such difficult lives, both now

and twenty years ago, the time I first started thinking about this idea. They stumble in the race to get the "right" education, they're crushed by friendships based on classroom hierarchies, they suffer from the excessive meddling or outright neglect of their parents—the list of issues they face is endless. Bullying. Dropping out. Suicide. All these many painful challenges that accompany teen years brought up a question for me when I specialized in children's literature: What could a novel possibly do in the face of this grave reality?

I could write the serious reality seriously. That's certainly one way. But these young people have their hands full already with their own problems and cannot push themselves to care about the difficult situation endured by some stranger in a book. Besides, for those who aren't in the habit of reading, just following the letters on the page is a struggle.

I chose to write about a serious subject with a comical touch, I chose to depict it lightly. I wanted kids who liked reading and those who didn't to have fun with it to start. I wanted them to laugh and roll their eyes at and relate to everything the characters did. I wanted them to enter the world of the book and be free of their everyday lives. And then, when they closed the book at the end, I wanted the weight on their hearts to be just a little lighter.

Afterword

I don't know if I succeeded in that, but ever since *Colorful* was first published, many younger readers and their families have reached out to me with unforgettable messages. There was the girl who confessed to me: "I stopped thinking about suicide after I read *Colorful*." And the mother who told me: "My daughter used to lock herself in her room every day and refuse to go to school at all, but after she read *Colorful*, she started going again." I've heard from a great number of people how *Colorful* became an opportunity for change.

To really dig into the why of it, I think all the problems start with the inescapable truth that we are who we are. The more sincere the person, the more deeply they look into their own hearts, and they end up exhausted. The idea I present in *Colorful*—about becoming a different person and living life over again—perhaps allows such readers to feel the relief of getting some distance from themselves.

I think the issue of young people struggling and growing tired of the world before they have the chance to truly know it isn't limited to Japan. Neither is the draining fight against a closed-off society in which the air grows more stagnant with each passing year.

My sincerest hope is that *Colorful* goes beyond national

Afterword

boundaries and also provides this same breath of fresh air for American readers.

I am deeply grateful to all the people who have worked so hard to make the English version of *Colorful* a reality, but especially to my translator Jocelyne Allen.

ETO MORI

© Toshiharu Sakai

ETO MORI has been a literary star in Japan for over thirty years. She has won numerous major awards in Japan, including the Naoki Prize, one of Japan's most prestigious awards for popular fiction. *Colorful* has been translated into seven languages and adapted into three films. *Colorful* is her first novel to be translated into English. She lives in Tokyo, Japan.

© Christopher Butcher

JOCELYNE ALLEN has translated hundreds of short stories, novels, and manga, including the Eisner Award–winning titles *Frankenstein* by Junji Ito and *Onward Towards Our Noble Deaths* by Shigeru Mizuki. She splits her time between Toronto and Tokyo.